3/05

Devil on
My Heels

Devil on
My Heels

Joyce McDonald

Delacorte Press

Published by
Delacorte Press
an imprint of
Random House Children's Books
a division of Random House, Inc.
New York

Visit us on the Web! www.randomhouse.com/teens
Educators and librarians, for a variety of teaching tools, visit us at
www.randomhouse.com/teachers

Library of Congress Cataloging-in-Publication Data
McDonald, Joyce.
Devil on my heels / Joyce McDonald.
p. cm.
Summary: In 1959 fifteen-year-old Dove, the daughter of a prosperous orange
grower in Benevolence, Florida, feels increasingly uneasy after learning of acts of
racism against the African American orange pickers by those close to her.
ISBN 0-385-73107-8 (trade)—ISBN 0-385-90133-X (GLB)
[1. Race relations—Fiction. 2. Racism—Fiction. 3. African Americans—
Fiction. 4. Migrant labor—Fiction. 5. Florida—History—20th century—
Fiction.] I. Title.
PZ7.M14817 De 2004 [Fic]—dc22
2003014474

The text of this book is set in 10.5-point Dutch 809.

Book design by Angela Carlino

Printed in the United States of America

May 2004

10 9 8 7 6 5 4 3 2 1

BVG

For my soul mate, Mac, who listens

• • • • • • • • • • • • • • •

With special thanks to Elvira Woodruff, who knows a thing or two
about reading poems in cemeteries

Lately I have taken to reading poems to dead boys in the Benevolence Baptist Cemetery. They don't walk away before I have finished the first sentence, like most of the live boys I know. When I read to them, their eyes don't wander to something, or someone, more interesting. I can pretend these boys are listening. I can pretend they hear me.

On Friday afternoons like this one, right after seventh period, I head straight for the cemetery. I like to sit beneath the Austrian pines in the cool shade, reading lines from Tennyson or Wordsworth, listening to the whisper of the wind through the branches—listening to the trees making up their own poems. Soft words in the language of wind and pine needles.

Miss Delpheena Poyer, my English teacher, is the reason I am sitting in the Baptist cemetery reading poems to dead boys. This marking period we are studying poetry. All kinds of poetry. A few weeks back Miss Poyer sent us on a mission to find interesting epitaphs on gravestones. That was our homework assignment. I went to three church cemeteries in Benevolence looking for verses. My favorite epitaph is engraved on the headstone of Rowena Mae Cunningham, who died in 1871, wife of Cyril Cunningham.

HERE LIES ROWENA MAE

MY WIFE FOR 37 YEARS.

AND THIS IS THE FIRST DAMN THING

SHE EVER DONE TO OBLIGE ME.

I think that says all that needs to be said about the Cunninghams' marriage.

This afternoon I am reading to Charles Henry Colewater, "Beloved son of Emily and Carter Colewater," who died at the age of fourteen in 1903. He was only a year younger than I am now. His parents' graves are to the right of his. Sometimes I have this eerie feeling their spirits are hovering over my shoulder, making sure I don't read anything they'd disapprove of. This is, after all, a Baptist cemetery.

I lean my shoulder against Charles Henry's headstone. If I close my eyes, I can imagine I see his face, a friendly face dotted with light freckles across his nose and cheeks, like little muddy footprints left behind by ants.

My mom's grave is only a few yards from Charles Henry's. All it says on her headstone is *Caroline Winfield Alderman,*

1922–1947, wife of Lucas Alderman. It doesn't say a word about her being mother to Dove Alderman. I was barely four years old when she left this earth, so I don't remember her very well. But it makes me a little sad that nobody took the time to write an epitaph for her.

This week in Miss Poyer's class we are studying sonnets. I flip through the *Selected Poems of John Keats*, pick out one of his sonnets, and start right in reading it to Charles Henry. Only, the first line stops me cold: "When I have fears that I may cease to be." I know those fears Keats is talking about. Sometimes I lie awake half the night, worrying that Mr. Khrushchev and those Soviets might decide to drop an atom bomb right smack-dab in the middle of Florida before I know what a real kiss feels like. Not those slobbery head-on collisions after the bottle stops spinning, with everybody looking on. I mean the real thing. Although I'm a little vague on what that might be.

Not that I haven't been kissed a few times. I have. Even been French kissed by Bobby McNeill in eighth grade at Donna Redfern's party when we were dancing and somebody turned the lights out. I was expecting a plain old spin-the-bottle kiss. The next thing I knew, I thought I had a raw oyster stuck in my mouth.

I am absolutely positive that kissing gets better than this. Otherwise I would lie down right here next to Charles Henry and pull the sod up over my head.

I rest my shoulder against the chiseled curve of his tombstone. Poor Charles Henry. He was so young when he died. This is why I read poems—love poems mostly—to boys like him, boys who most likely passed on before they ever had a chance to fall in love. If I were in their shoes, I would certainly be most appreciative of any visitors stopping by my final resting place to read a poem to me now and then.

A wind suddenly kicks up its heels and tears the pages from my hand as I'm flipping through *Selected Poems*, trying to find something a little more cheerful to read to Charles Henry. It sets the Spanish moss into frenzied flapping over head in the trees. A storm is coming. They have a way of springing up unannounced on steamy afternoons in Florida.

A loud crash of thunder rumbles through the trees, sending me to my feet. Dark clouds tumble all over each other. I smell the rain in the air, a chilled metallic smell, even sense it on my skin. But I can't see it. It is as if the rain is stuck in some kind of purgatory between the earth and the sky.

The Austrian pines have stopped their whispering and are beginning to moan—loud eerie moans that burrow into my bones. The first bolt of lightning makes a beeline for the woods behind the church.

The sky turns the color of lead. Everything around me blurs into tones of gray, except for a large splotch of red in the distance. The red splotch zips along a few feet above the earth, picking up speed. A flash of lightning outlines everything in sharp blinding white. I recognize that faded red T-shirt and the person wearing it. I watch him stop to fold something and stuff it into his back pocket. Then he takes off running through the cemetery toward the road.

I don't move from my place beside Charles Henry. When the blob of red is only a few yards from me, it stops. We stare at each other. The wind blows sand in my eyes, making them tear.

"Gator?" I shout above the roar. This is what goes through my mind faster than the next bolt of lightning can streak to the ground: *Why aren't you in the groves picking oranges? Travis Waite is going to fire your hide for sure if he hasn't already. And what, for heaven's sake, are you doing in a cemetery that's for white folks in the middle of the afternoon with lightning bolts looking for any moving target in sight?*

I shout his name again, but Gator doesn't answer. The wind beats at his red T-shirt as if it is trying to tear it right off his body.

The thunder seeps into the soles of my penny loafers. It rumbles through my body. I pick up my books, tuck them close to my chest, and keep my head down. I have to find someplace to get away from the storm. I head across the cemetery, walking as fast as I can in a pencil-straight skirt with nothing but a tiny kick pleat for maneuvering.

By now the wind has whipped itself into a frenzy. Flying sand stings my legs. A streak of lightning zigzags into the meadow across the street. When I look back, the red shirt is gone. Gator has disappeared.

This is what I am puzzling over, in between rumbles of thunder, when I hear another sound: the piercing honk of a car horn. I look up to see Chase Tully, grinning at me from his silver-blue T-bird convertible.

Chase Tully is one of those boys whose eyes glaze over whenever I try to read him a poem. Although the last time I tried to do that was four years ago.

Chase leans into the steering wheel and shouts, "Come on, Dove, get in! You'll get soaked."

Back when we were kids I would have yelled something smart-alecky at him, like "Well, riding in a convertible with someone dumb enough to leave the top down in the middle of a storm isn't exactly my idea of an improvement." I don't say that now. The truth is, even though I've known him all my life, I'm not sure how to act around Chase anymore.

Chase and I practically grew up together. Our fathers'

groves bump right up against each other. Jacob Tully has over a thousand acres, the most groves of anybody in all of Panther County. My dad has about seven hundred.

Chase and I used to play in my dad's groves every chance we got. If I had something on my mind, Chase was usually the first to hear it. Straight out, no holds barred. Back then, he was about as wide as a yardstick, with these large ears and a goofy-looking crew cut.

Then he went and turned thirteen and everything changed.

For the next three years he acted as if he couldn't remember my name. Depending on the occasion, I was Twerp or Squirt—usually in front of his girlfriends. Around the guys he hung out with I was Spaz or Kid. The rest of the time he made up whatever name struck his fancy: Mouse, Noodlehead, Beanpole. The list was irritatingly endless.

It wasn't until I came to Benevolence High last year that he finally stopped calling me names and telling me to get lost every chance he got, and started giving me that lazy grin of his again. He still teases me, though, which is why I don't know what to make of him these days.

The wind cranks it up a notch, pushing me away from the car. "Come on!" Chase shouts over the thunder. He lifts his leather jacket from the passenger seat and tosses it in the back.

The top whirs as it climbs up from the back of the car. Chase reaches up and locks it in place.

Drops of rain tickle my arms and run down my nose. I hunch over my books, trying to keep them dry just as the sky opens up and sends a waterfall roaring down on my head.

Like any sensible person, I lunge for the door handle and slide into the soft leather bucket seat.

Chase glances in the rearview mirror and smooths the sides of his dark hair back with his hands. He's got sideburns now. No more crew cut. And his body finally caught up to those ears.

He flicks on the windshield wipers but keeps his foot on the brake. We sit there with the engine purring. "So, where we headed?" He doesn't look at me. His eyes are glued to the dashboard. He licks his thumb and rubs at a smudge of dirt by the radio.

"Just home," I say.

He grins and shakes his head. "That's it? Home?" He reaches across my lap and opens the glove compartment. A whole pile of road maps tumbles out. "Dove, jeez, where's your imagination?"

For as far back as I can remember, Chase has had the largest collection of maps of any person I've ever met. Probably more than the whole state of Florida put together. He reads maps the way other kids read comic books.

"Take your pick," he says.

"I already did," I tell him. "Or weren't you listening?"

He drapes his arm across the back of my seat and starts playing with my damp hair while I pick up the maps and stuff them back in the glove compartment. I don't have to look in the rearview mirror to know that for all the hair spray I used this morning my hair is now a mess of dark bedsprings. When we were kids, Chase used to tease me, saying I had hair like colored folks, especially when it got wet. I didn't need him or anybody else to make me feel bad about my hair. I could do that all by myself just by looking in the mirror.

Chase's fingers have wandered down to the back of my neck, sending little shivers up and down my spine. I don't let on, though. I know he's only teasing me. I shove his hand away. "If you don't get this car moving, I'm going to get out and walk, rain or no rain."

He laughs, then lifts his foot off the brake. The car jerks forward. "You hear about Silas Beaureve's groves getting torched last night?" he asks.

"That's all anybody was talking about in homeroom this morning," I say. Silas Beaureve has one of the smaller groves in the area, about a hundred acres. I look over at Chase. "Somebody said he lost about two acres."

"Half acre."

"Lightning, you think?"

"Maybe."

"Probably was."

"Been a lot of lightning hits around here lately," he says.

It's like somebody has taken to sliding ice cubes up and down my arms. I rub them to get rid of the goose bumps.

Chase isn't saying anything everybody else isn't already thinking. The fires started a few weeks back with Moss Henley's outhouse going up in flames. Everybody thought it was a good joke on Moss. A week later Travis Waite's toolshed caught fire. Folks figured it was probably an accident, gasoline leaking from the lawn mower or something. Then the bleachers over by the football field burned down and people started to worry. Now, with Silas Beaureve's orange groves getting torched—although I am still holding to the lightning theory myself—people have begun looking around for somebody to blame.

9

"They're saying it might be one of the pickers," Chase says. "Maybe more than one."

"Well, now, that doesn't make much sense. They need the work. Why would they burn down Silas's groves right in the middle of picking season?" I bend down to get one of the maps I missed and return it to the glove compartment. "And that doesn't explain those other fires."

"Doesn't it? Think about it. Moss is on the police force. And he's friends with Travis Waite. Travis is the crew boss for most of the pickers around here." Chase says this like he knows something I don't.

"So?"

"Maybe there's some connection. Somebody out to cause trouble, to get revenge or something."

"Well, sure. Revenge. Probably one of the pickers burned down the bleachers because some cheerleader wouldn't go out with him." I grin at Chase. He doesn't notice.

After that we don't talk for the next three blocks. The car picks up speed as we head onto the county road toward home. Chase has the wipers going full blast, but the rain is so heavy I can't see through the windshield.

I'm getting worried. If I can't see the road, then how can he? My heart has picked up the beat of the wipers. *Swishthunkswishthunkswishthunk.* I am having Keatsian fears of ceasing to be.

"Maybe you should pull over until the rain lets up," I tell him.

Chase ignores me. No surprise there.

"Well, for heaven's sake, slow down, then."

He lightens his foot on the gas pedal.

With all this talk about the pickers, I suddenly remember Gator. I look over at Chase. "You see anybody besides me in the cemetery when you pulled up?"

He shakes his head. "No. Why?"

I shrug.

"What were you doing in the cemetery?"

Drat. I knew I shouldn't have brought that up. I'm not about to tell him I've been reading poems to dead boys. "English assignment," I say.

"Delpheena Poyer."

It isn't a question, but I nod anyway.

"Epitaphs."

Another nod. Chase had Miss Poyer two years earlier. He doesn't have to know the assignment was weeks ago.

I've got Gator stuck in my head. Gator has been working in our groves since he wasn't much higher than my dad's knee. He shows up every season, as reliable as lightning bugs in April. Nobody knows who he belongs to, if anybody. Seems like most of the pickers look out for him while he's here—or used to when he was a kid—but as far as I know, no one's ever claimed him. Nobody even knows for sure how old he is, not even Gator himself. I figure him to be about the same age as Chase, probably eighteen.

When we were kids, Gator used to play with Chase and me in my dad's groves. Sometimes we would climb the trees right to the top and pretend we were up in the mast of a huge sailing ship, looking out over our green sea. Those trees were our spaceships, our pirate ships, and our whaling ships. They were always taking us to faraway places, like China or India or Africa. Or Mars, if we happened to be playing Flash Gordon.

Gator liked the pirate games the best. Sometimes we played *Treasure Island* and Gator always insisted on being Long John Silver. He'd carry a big walking stick, pretending it was a crutch stuck under his arm, and hop around on one leg.

Chase liked playing in our groves better than in his own, which made sense, considering his dad, Jacob Tully, was forever yelling at us about one thing or another. He sure as heck didn't like us playing with Gator or any of the pickers' kids. As for my dad, he didn't seem to notice us playing with Gator. That's because after my mom died, my dad left most of the child rearing up to our housekeeper, Delia Washburn. He's never paid much attention to what I do unless I get in trouble.

Whenever anybody tried to tell the three of us we weren't supposed to be playing together, we just took off for another part of the groves and kept right on with our games. Until this one day Jacob Tully made a point of telling my dad. My dad took Chase and me aside and told us it wasn't a good idea, us playing with the hired help, especially when they were supposed to be working. He said we'd get Gator in trouble with his crew boss. I was maybe seven at the time. Gator couldn't have been more than ten.

I remember crawling under one of the orange trees and crying while Chase told Gator we couldn't play with him anymore. From then on we played in parts of the groves where the pickers weren't working so as not to make Gator feel bad. It was never the same after that, playing those games without Gator.

Chase is fiddling with the radio. I stare at his hand on the tuner and wonder if he ever thinks about those times. Did he miss Gator as much as I did after we stopped playing with him? Chase never talked about it. And I never asked.

We are about a half mile from the turnoff to my house. There hasn't been any rain here at all, which is the way it is sometimes. A few minutes later we are raising clouds of dust, tearing up the dirt road that becomes our driveway and curves around in front of our house.

I'm trying to decide whether to invite Chase in for some iced tea or something when he says, "Gotta go. I'm meeting some friends over at Whelan's." Whelan's Drive-In is the local after-school hangout. Chase reaches across me and opens the door. Suddenly I get this crazy notion in my head. I want to grab his hand before he lets go of the door handle. Instead I stumble out of the car, mumbling, "Thanks for the ride." But I don't think he hears me with the radio blasting as he peels down our dirt road.

I toss my books on the front-porch rocker and head around back. Our dirt driveway continues on behind our house and leads to the groves.

I'm trying my best not to think about wanting to reach for Chase's hand and his being in such an all-fired hurry to drop me off and leave. A breeze rustles the leaves of the orange trees. I push thoughts of Chase out of my head and let the scent of orange blossoms fill me up. It is Valencia season. Orange trees, thick with dark green leaves, glossy yellow-white blossoms, and clusters of oranges, surround me. That's what I love best about Valencias—the trees have blossoms and fruit on them at the same time.

Sometimes, when I stand still in this place, it's as if I'm melting into the air. For the tiniest moment everything seems to be as it should. Not good or bad, ugly or beautiful. Just what it is. Nowhere else on earth do I get this feeling.

The dirt is soft and sandy. It spills up over the sides of my loafers. If you aren't careful you can sink right up to your shins. I take off one loafer at a time and shake it out. After that I keep to the tractor ruts where the dirt is packed down.

I reach a crossroad and stand there for a few minutes, deciding which way to go. Up ahead Travis Waite is digging through one of the orange crates, probably checking to make sure nobody is cheating my dad by hiding bad fruit. The pickers are paid by the crate, so sometimes they hide spoiled fruit on the bottom. But not very often. Most of our pickers are honest, hardworking folks.

With any luck at all, Travis will be too busy to notice me. He doesn't like me talking to the pickers because it slows them down.

Some of the younger kids come running up when they see me. Most of them are barefoot and not wearing much besides ratty old pants and dirty T-shirts.

I know a couple of them by name: Teak and Jody and a few others. But there are also a lot of new faces. Three small boys, probably not older than six or seven, pass me, lugging a wooden ladder. It takes all of them and one older boy, who comes over to help, to lean it up against one of the orange trees.

The ladders are twenty feet high, wide at the bottom and narrow at the top. They aren't the easiest things to haul around. Once, a few years back, I tried to move one of those ladders just a few inches and it toppled over on me. It about cracked my skull open. I had a knot the size of a golf ball on my forehead for a week.

Some of the kids skip backward a few feet ahead, keeping their eyes on me. I wonder how many of them, if any, went to school today. Education is a little spotty for most of the migrant kids. They sometimes help their folks with the picking instead of going to school. The more crates they fill, the more money their families make, which isn't much. But my dad says at least they're making an honest living and not looking for handouts.

I look around, but I don't see Gator. Old Eli is up ahead, though. Eli has been working in our groves since before I was born. He isn't a seasonal worker like the others. He oversees the pruning and spraying, the weeding—all the things that have to be done to make sure you get a good crop. And when the oranges are ready, he sometimes helps with the picking. Eli is darn proud of being a fruit picker. He told me once how his family has never done stoop labor, which is picking row crops.

Eli empties the oranges from his sack and heads back up the ladder to pick some more. The strap of the large canvas bag hangs over his shoulder and across his chest. The bag bumps against his hip as he climbs. His hands are as dark as chestnuts and as wrinkled and tough as walnut shells, but they're fast. Fruit seems to fly off that tree. He goes right on tossing oranges into his sack while he nods my way.

"Well, Miss Dove. Nice to see you out here." He pinches the brim of his cap in greeting. "You ain't been around much lately."

I shade my eyes and look up at him. "Not for a while," I say.

The pickers were at our groves late last fall when the other oranges were ready. Then they came back at the end of March when the Valencias needed picking. I haven't been in the groves at all this season.

Eli is watching me. His eyes have heavy, half-closed lids that make him look as if he's weary to the bone. "Well, you a young lady now. Too old to be playing in the groves."

"He's right, Miss Dove. You shouldn't be out here by yourself."

I smell Travis Waite before I see his face. He comes up from behind and stands next to me, watching Eli. His jaw rolls in slow circles as he chews his wad of tobacco. What I smell, though, isn't tobacco. It's whiskey. That surprises me.

This is a dry county. You have to go over the county line if you want anything stronger than beer. Travis Waite might raise hell on the weekends, hitting the beer joints with his buddies, tearing through the dirt roads in his pickup, shooting at any poor animal that moves, but in all the years he has worked for us, I've never known him to drink on the job. Or maybe I just never noticed.

Travis stands there, rubbing his beard stubble with the back of his hand. Everybody in Benevolence knows Travis Waite is one of the best crew bosses around. My dad has been dealing with him for years. They went to school together. Even played on the football team together, along with Chase's dad. But that doesn't mean I have to like him. And to be honest, I don't. Standing less than three feet from him has set my skin to crawling on more than one occasion.

Eli nods at Travis as he backs down the ladder with his full canvas bag, rustling the glossy leaves on his way. He pulls the drawstring at the bottom and oranges tumble into the wooden bin. He looks over at us and smiles, showing off the dark gaps where some of his teeth used to be.

Another picker is sitting down, leaning against one of the crates. He has his back to me, but I know right off it's Gator. His threadbare dungarees have holes in both knees and his faded red T-shirt is still damp from the rain. I'm relieved to see him. Although I can't for the life of me figure out how he got back here so fast.

He's sitting with his knees pulled up, sketching something on brown paper with a piece of charcoal. Delia saves paper sacks from the grocery store for Gator to draw on. She's been doing this for as long as I can remember.

I walk over to see what he's drawing. It's a picture of Eli up on his ladder. Gator's captured something in Eli's expression. Whatever it is, it makes me proud to know Eli.

"Hey, Gator," I say.

He looks back over his shoulder and gives me a nod. Neither of us says anything about his being in the cemetery.

Travis creeps up beside him. He nudges Gator's hip with the toe of his boot. "This ain't no art school."

"I'm taking a break." Gator squints up at Eli, who is heading back up the ladder, and draws a few more lines.

"You want to work on my crew, then you'd better get moving."

"I get paid for what I pick," Gator says. "I can decide for myself how much money I want to make." He glances up from his drawing. There is something disturbing about the look in his eyes when he stares at his crew boss.

"Yeah? Well, it just so happens I also get paid for what *you* pick. And if somebody in my crew ain't pulling his weight, then I'll find somebody who will." Travis sends a stream of tobacco juice Gator's way, missing his bare feet by a hair. He points to the top of the tree next to Gator. "You got a bunch of shiners up there." Shiners are oranges the pickers have missed. They stick out like bright lightbulbs.

Gator jams the charcoal in his back pocket. He gets to his feet, slowly rolls up the brown paper, and tucks it in his other back pocket. He never once looks at Travis. Without a word he walks over to one of the other trees, picks up his canvas sack where he left it, and climbs the ladder.

The thing about Gator is that he has this kind of unhurried, prideful way of carrying himself, which bothers some folks, him being colored and all. But I've never minded. I guess people think he isn't being respectful or something. Mostly I think it's because he doesn't even notice them.

Travis grabs the shiner pole. My first thought is that he's going to throttle Gator with it. But he just flicks off the few oranges left behind on the tree. They hit the ground with dull thuds.

"You need a ride back to the house, Miss Dove?"

I can't figure why Travis Waite is so all-fired anxious to get me away from here. All I want to do is walk through the groves for a while. "No thanks," I tell him.

"Don't mean no disrespect, Miss Dove, but I think it would be best if you got on home." Travis is watching me; his dull squinty eyes put me in mind of dried peas. They lock onto mine. It's as if he is willing me to understand something and save him the embarrassment of having to spell it all out for me, which I am not about to do.

Travis lifts his ratty old baseball cap and scratches the top of his head. His dark hair is plastered to his scalp with oily sweat. "Your daddy won't like you being out here alone, Miss Dove. Being out here by yourself . . . well, now . . . it's asking for—"

He stops and jerks his thumb toward the tree where Gator is picking Valencias. "I don't want you putting yourself in any dangerous situations is all."

Danger? I've been playing in these groves most of my life. Suddenly Eli's words about my being a young lady take on a whole new meaning. I don't like what Travis is insinuating, that I'm not safe in my own groves anymore.

It is almost five-thirty, but the sun is still bright. "I'm not finished taking my walk yet," I tell Travis as I head on down the dirt road, going deeper into the groves.

When I'm no longer in his line of vision, I slip behind a row of orange trees. I snap orange blossoms from a lower branch and tuck them behind my ear. I kick off my gritty loafers, unhook my stockings from my garter belt, and slip them off. The sand warms the soles of my feet and the spaces between my toes.

If I were still a kid, I would rip off my narrow skirt with its tiny kick pleat the way I used to toss aside my overalls and polo shirt. I would take off running and leaping between the trees. Wild and free. If I were still a kid, I would do it in a heartbeat.

4

Delia throws sausage into the cast-iron skillet. Grease rains over the stove. She has on an old pair of painter's coveralls, a T-shirt, and black high-top sneakers that make her look more like one of the pickers than our housekeeper. Actually, they're her husband Gus's coveralls. Ever since he got himself killed in a hit-and-run a few years back, Delia has taken to wearing his clothes.

I asked her about that once. She said it wasn't any of my business what she wore or why she wore it. End of conversation.

Delia nods her good morning.

Overhead the ceiling fan makes scraping sounds as it

whirls. It's not even ten o'clock and Delia already has three fans going in the kitchen. That's how I always know, without bothering to turn on the radio, that we're in for a scorcher.

I slide into the chair across the table from my dad. He's got his face in some dusty old account ledger. Bills are stacked beside his plate like piles of those skinny French pancakes. In between scribbling numbers into a column, he takes a bite of grits dripping with egg yolk. He chews. He studies an invoice. He writes in the ledger. He forks another mouthful of eggs and grits. He chews some more. My dad has been known to take up to two hours to eat breakfast. I know this from Delia. I've never actually stuck around long enough to find out if it's true.

"Morning, Dad," I say.

He looks up from the ledger and grins at me. He's got dimples so deep you could lose the whole tip of your finger in them. "Mornin', sugar."

This is about the extent of our conversation each morning. We usually don't have much to say to each other.

Dad stretches his arms out in front of him and cracks his knuckles a few times. His hands are wide, with long, bony fingers and knuckles the size of large marbles.

Delia comes up behind me and scrapes sausage, bacon, and two eggs over easy onto my plate. I plunge my fork into my eggs just as somebody knocks at the back door. My dad doesn't seem to notice. He's too busy adding up figures.

Delia swings open the screen door and Travis Waite steps into the kitchen. He takes off his sweat-stained cap and gives Dad and me a crooked smile, exposing brown tobacco-stained teeth. I stare down at my eggs. The runny yolk has started to congeal.

Travis tells my dad he needs to see him outside.

I keep my head down. I shove my food around the plate with my fork, putting everything in order. Sausage at eight o'clock. Bacon at twelve. Eggs at four. I reach for a hot biscuit, butter it, and watch the butter melt. It runs over the side and oozes into the palm of my hand. I lick it off.

The screen door bangs once, then twice. When I look up, Delia and I are alone. We stare across the room at each other. We both know Travis wouldn't interrupt my dad's breakfast unless there was trouble.

I slide my chair back. Before I'm even on my feet, Delia says, "You just keep that backside of yours right where it is."

"You want to know what's going on as much as I do."

"Travis Waite didn't come here asking to talk to you, did he?"

"Something's going on."

Delia pours the grease from the skillet into an empty coffee can. I watch her hands. The skillet is heavy, but the pan doesn't even wobble as she chips away at the crusted bottom with the spatula. "If it's something you need to know, your daddy'll tell you." She stabs the spatula in my direction. A few drops of grease splatter on the linoleum. "Your breakfast's gettin' cold."

Delia and I have been having these battles of wills since the day I learned my first word: *beans*. Delia leaned right into my face, lifted the green mush from the baby-food jar, and pointed to it. "They're peas, baby girl. Not beans."

"Beans," I said. "Beansbeansbeans." I went right on saying that word until Delia held up a roll of adhesive tape and threatened to seal my mouth shut, temporarily putting an end to my defiance.

My own recollection of this momentous event, which happened when I was barely a toddler, is nonexistent. My dad is the one who likes telling the story. He's got a whole stock of stories about our wars—Delia's and mine. But he's never taken sides in them.

Delia is eyeing me, trying to size up what my next move is going to be. I brush a few biscuit crumbs from my Bermuda shorts and pick up my fork. It's not worth the effort, arguing over something I can wheedle out of my dad when he gets back.

Only, he doesn't come back.

I go upstairs to read my latest issue of *Seventeen*. When I come back down an hour later, Delia is dumping the food from my dad's plate into the trash.

I've got an appointment to get my hair cut at noon. Then I'm supposed to meet my friend Rayanne Beecham at the movie theater. My dad hasn't given me my allowance yet. And it is a two-mile walk to town. I have been hoping he will give me a ride. It's not like I can't walk that distance. I do it all the time. But it is already eighty-five degrees outside and the air is so humid it makes my lungs feel spongy.

I run back upstairs and check my wallet. Three dollars. My haircut is going to cost a dollar fifty, plus the tip. The matinee costs fifty cents. I do the math in my head. If I don't get popcorn, I can stop by Whelan's Drive-In after the movie for a Coke and maybe a hot dog or hamburger. My only problem at the moment is finding a ride. I decide I've still got time.

I file my nails and try out my new nail polish. The exact same shade of shell-pink pearl that the model on the cover of *Seventeen* is wearing.

When it's almost noon, I stand at the top of the stairs and listen. Silence. "Dad?" I shout. "You down there?" Nothing. "Delia?" Delia doesn't answer either.

I have no idea where she's got to. But if I don't get moving, I'll miss my hair appointment. There is nothing left to do but grab my purse and start walking.

* * * * * * * * * * * * * * * * * *

By the time I get to Luellen's beauty shop I am twenty minutes late and feeling like one big drop of water. My blouse sticks to my back and sweat dribbles down the sides of my face. My hair is a hopeless helmet of frizz.

Luellen is snipping away at Erdine Tucker's hair while Erdine sips an RC Cola. Erdine is a senior. She gives me a floppy wave when I come through the door.

Luellen has a waiting area set up in one corner of her beauty shop. I take a seat and flip through *HairDo* magazine. That gets old real quick. You can spend just so long staring at photos of models who all look like they belong in a Breck shampoo ad.

Some girl I've never seen before is busy sudsing up Marilee Redfern's hair in the sink across the room. Mrs. Redfern is Judge Redfern's wife and head of the school board.

The girl has her own hair pulled back in a ponytail. She's not much more than a little slip of a thing.

The front of her uniform has large splotches of water on it. Luellen makes everybody who works for her wear uniforms—light blue with white Peter Pan collars and white aprons. They look like waitress uniforms.

Luellen's face is shiny with perspiration. Little strands of red-brown curls stick to her cheeks. She brushes them away with the back of her hand. "Phew, it's hotter than a griddle in Hades out there today. You want another RC, Erdine, honey?"

Erdine shakes her head. "I'm fine, thanks."

"How about you, Dove?" Luellen calls over to me.

I shake my head. "No thanks. You sure could do with an air conditioner, Luellen," I tell her. "Folks don't want to spend money getting their hair done on a day like this. Their do'll flop before they even make it through your front door." I don't bother to mention that my legs are stuck to the turquoise plastic seat cover.

Luellen nods. "Well, now, you got a point, Dove. It's just them things is so darn expensive. My electric bill would go through the roof."

"A ceiling fan might be nice," Erdine offers. She points toward Luellen's ceiling and takes a long swallow of her RC.

I am watching Erdine in the mirror when I catch a glimpse of Luellen's hair washer staring at me. When I turn around to look at her, she goes back to rinsing the last of the soap out of Mrs. Redfern's hair. Even after all that shampooing, I can still smell the lotion from her permanent wave all the way across the room.

The girl wraps Mrs. Redfern's hair in a pink towel and sends her over to Luellen. Then she leans over the sink and rinses away the soap bubbles. Spidery wisps of pale hair escape from her ponytail and fall across her cheeks. She has skinny arms covered with light freckles. I can't help but wonder where she's from. We don't get many folks moving into Benevolence.

The girl picks up a towel to dry her hands. She gives me a shy smile. I notice a dark gap where's she's missing a tooth on the upper right side of her mouth. She reaches for the broom and sweeps up hair that has formed a little nest around one of the empty chairs.

Erdine admires her haircut in the mirror while Luellen unties the cloth that has been covering Erdine's clothes and dumps the hair on the floor.

I'm getting worried. If Mrs. Redfern is next in line, I'll never make it to the movie theater in time. Usually Luellen has at least two people working with her on Saturdays, not counting the hair-washing person.

Just when I am thinking I might have to cancel my appointment, here comes Nona Parker from the back room. She brushes powdered sugar from around her bright red lipstick mouth, smearing a little red to one side. Her uniform is stretched so tight across her chest, the buttons look about ready to pop off.

Nona is okay with perms and setting hair, but her haircutting skills are sorely lacking. I do not want her to come anywhere near me with a pair of scissors. Silently I say a prayer that Nona will set Mrs. Redfern's hair, leaving Luellen to cut mine.

Apparently the Lord is on vacation and doesn't get my message because Nona is suddenly looming over me. She practically pulls me to my feet and steers me toward one of the chairs, the whole time talking a blue streak about how long it's been since they last saw me, and oh my, wasn't my hair having a frizzy fit today. Nona stands close to six feet tall in her stocking feet and weighs at least seventy-five pounds more than I do. She is not someone you want to offend, especially when she is packing a pair of scissors.

I plop into the chair and stare over at Luellen, trying to get her attention. I send her desperate eye signals: *Save me, Luellen, and I promise I will always come to your shop to get my hair cut no matter where I'm living, even if I have to travel halfway around the world to get here.*

Erdine gets out of her chair and brushes off her capri pants, even though there isn't a single strand of hair on them. We both look into the mirror at the same time. Then she leans over and whispers, "Her folks are . . ." Erdine stops talking and blinks a few times, like her batteries have died or something.

"Are what?"

"Well, you know . . . migrants." What Erdine doesn't say, I hear in the way she says *migrants*. What she means is "white trash."

At first I think she's talking about Nona. But this can't be, because Nona has grown up in this town. She graduated from our high school five or six years ago. Her father owns the Gulf station at the far end of Main Street.

Erdine picks up on my confusion. "I'm talking about the girl—what's her name?—Rosemary something." She tilts her head toward where the new girl is now washing plastic perm curlers in the sink and stacking them in a pile on a towel.

Nona pins her fists to her hips and practically snorts at Erdine. "Aren't you about done here?" she says.

Erdine straightens up and pulls her shoulders back. She turns to Luellen, who's busy winding rollers into Mrs. Redfern's hair. "I'll just leave my money up front by the register," she says. Without waiting to see what Luellen has to say about that, she marches to the front door, plunking down a dollar and some change on her way out.

I glance at my watch. I've got less than fifteen minutes to get to the movie theater.

5

Never ask a hairdresser if she can "hurry it up a bit." Even if you're desperate and worried your best friend is going to strangle you for making her late for a movie she's been waiting months to see. Fortunately the shock of my hair is enough to make Rayanne forget I'm late, at least for the moment.

"What in the Sam Hill kind of hairdo is that?" she says, reaching for what little hair I have left. She tugs at a frizzy lock. "Wait! Who's that colored man used to dance with Shirley Temple in the movies? Oh, I know! Bojangles. You got yourself a Bojangles haircut."

I smack her hand away from my hair. "It's not *that* short." Rayanne's perfect blond pageboy with not one strand out of place is only making things worse. I want to shake my fingers through her hair till it's a tangled mess.

I glance over at the movie poster of Leslie Caron, with her hair all swirled up on top of her head, looking gorgeous as Gigi. And very French.

"It's kind of French-looking, don't you think?" I run my hand through my hair and toss my head back with what I hope is considerable dramatic flare. "Paris. Left Bank. Very artsy," I say, as if this is the look I was going for all along.

"Well, you do sort of resemble a French poodle."

"Think Audrey Hepburn in *Sabrina*."

"Except frizzy."

"The movie's already started," I remind her.

Rayanne looks at her watch and goes right off the deep end. "Oh Lord, we missed the cartoon!" she shrieks. She runs to the ticket window and throws a dollar at Wilma Boyd. "One, and hurry." Wilma looks over the top of her glasses at Rayanne and throws a ticket and two quarters right back at her. Wilma is not one to take any guff. I slip a dollar her way and she slides a ticket and my change over to me.

The theater is dark. Billy Tyler, the usher, is nowhere around to show us to our seats. We inch carefully down the aisle, searching for two empty chairs. The place is packed. We finally find two in the first row. In the glare of the light from the movie screen, I can see Rayanne scowling at me. She's got on her I'm-gonna-hate-you-till-I-die look. I pretend I don't notice.

Rayanne is squinting and rubbing her eyes when we step out into the lobby after the movie. "It's like I got somebody on the inside of my head trying to pop my eyeballs out of my sockets," she says. She's still trying to make me feel guilty about those front-row seats.

I'm doing a little squinting myself. All that afternoon sunlight coming through the glass doors is blinding. I don't care how many times I've been to the matinee, I always come out of the movie theater feeling like the world's been turned upside down. It takes me a while to get myself righted again.

Well, I have almost succeeded by the time I step outside, when I spot Rosemary Whatshername across the street in front of Tuckett's Hardware, which is next door to Luellen's. And the person standing there talking to her, like it was the most natural thing in the world, is Gator. Suddenly the whole world goes slap upside down again.

Rayanne tugs at my arm. She leans in close. I can smell jujubes on her breath. "Isn't that colored boy one of the pickers from your groves?"

"Gator," I breathe. I am watching Gator and Rosemary, and I am watching everybody around me watching them. Eyebrows arch. Lips shrivel into tight little lines. Gasps are swallowed before they can reach the air. Everybody knows colored boys do not have casual conversations with white girls on the streets of this town. They do not smile at them the way Gator is smiling at Rosemary. White girls do not giggle and cover their mouths with small freckled hands when colored boys say something funny. But Rosemary does just that.

"Oh, Dove," Rayanne whispers. "He shouldn't be talking to that girl. Doesn't he know any better?"

"I don't think it much matters to him," I tell her. I notice

Gator's not wearing the red T-shirt. He's got on dungarees without holes in the knees and a blue shirt with the sleeves rolled up partway. It looks new.

"He's just asking for trouble."

That's not what he's asking for, I want to say. But I don't. Because I know Rayanne is right.

"And why's that girl standing there letting him go on like that?" she asks.

Just then Gator shifts his eyes in my direction and I stop breathing. Wave after wave of heat rises from the sidewalk, encasing me in a bubble of hot air. I send Gator telepathic messages: *Don't nod at me. Don't say anything. Things are bad enough. Don't make them worse.*

My mind races ahead. What do I do if he talks to me? It's not as if I don't know the rules. But this is different. Gator works for us. Maybe nobody will think anything of it. Most folks in these parts know he's one of our pickers. They'll think he's just being respectful because I'm Lucas Alderman's daughter. I relax a little.

Gator locks his eyes on mine. I look down at the scorching pavement. At the curb. At popcorn somebody spilled in the gutter. A lizard slithers by and dives down the dark drain. I'd follow it if I could.

When I dare to look up, the danger has passed. Gator's attention is on Rosemary. He has decided to ignore me. I am suddenly a little put out about that. I am, after all, his employer's daughter.

"Well, what was that all about?" Rayanne says.

"What?"

"That Gator, watching you like that?"

"It's like you said. He's one of our pickers," I tell her. "He knows me is all."

People walking over by Tuckett's Hardware have taken to crossing to the other side of the street. Most of them pretend they aren't seeing what's happening right in front of their eyes on Main Street.

And they would have kept on pretending except that Willy Podd and Earl Hubbs, these two creeps who are a year ahead of me in school, come strutting around the corner. They stop in their tracks. Willy nudges Earl. They grin at each other and move closer.

Both are wearing black T-shirts. They hover around Gator and Rosemary, circling them like turkey buzzards.

About that time Chase Tully comes out of Tuckett's. He steps onto the sidewalk, leans his back against the brick wall, digs a crumpled pack of cigarettes from the pocket of his dungarees, slides out a cigarette, and takes his sweet time lighting it. He sucks in a long drag, exhales, and squints at the others through the smoke.

Willy nods at Chase, but Chase just stares right through him, like he's not even there.

By now Earl has his arm around Rosemary's shoulder. He makes it look as if he's trying to protect her, but I know better. Willy leans into her face. "This nigger bothering you, sugar?"

Rosemary's arms have been hanging limp and defenseless by her sides. Now her hands snap together. Her fingers lock, forming a tight fortress in front of what Delia would call her privates. She stares down at her sturdy white shoes—the ones Luellen makes her employees wear with their blue uniforms—and shakes her head. She whispers something to Willy.

Folks on both sides of Main Street have stopped walking. They are openly watching—a little too eagerly, maybe—to see what's going to happen. Although they already know how this is going to end. We all do. I pray that Willy and Earl let them go with nothing more than a few nasty remarks.

The Lord is apparently still on vacation because he doesn't catch this prayer, either. I no sooner send those words heavenward than Willy's leg shoots out, catching Gator in the back of the knees, knocking him off balance. At the same time, Earl gives Gator a hard shove from behind. Gator stumbles sideways. His head catches the brick wall, barely missing the plate-glass window of the hardware store before he lands on the sidewalk. Blood runs down the side of his face.

Without thinking I start across the street. Rayanne grabs my arm. "Stay out of this," she hisses. "What's the matter with you?" I know I should shake off her hand and try to help, but I don't. Part of me is maybe even a little grateful for her grip on me, although I don't much like admitting it.

Chase hasn't moved from his spot against the wall. He finishes his cigarette, tosses it to the sidewalk, and grinds it with his boot. For one hopeful second I think he is going to put a stop to this. But then he spots Rayanne and me. He's coming our way. Before he's halfway across the street, I yell, "Do something! Tell those creeps to lay off Gator!"

Chase cocks his head to one side and narrows his eyes at me. "Gator knows how to take care of himself."

"He's bleeding, for heaven's sake!" I shout at him. My

body is shaking from head to toe. "What is the *matter* with you?"

He looks over his shoulder at the crumpled heap that is Gator. "It's a head wound. Looks a lot worse than it is. He'll be okay." I can tell by the frown on his face that Chase isn't so sure about that.

Rosemary is trying to get to Gator. She has yanked off her white apron. It flaps in her hand like a flag of truce. But Earl grabs hold of her wrist and pulls her away.

The blood is awful. It is everywhere. Tiny streams of it spread, staining Gator's new shirt and his dungarees.

Rosemary is crying. She yanks her arm free from Earl's grip and ducks into Luellen's beauty shop. Willy gives Gator one good kick in the ribs, then joins Earl. The two of them look around, checking out their audience, and when they spot Chase, they head our way.

"Let's go," I say to Rayanne.

She ignores me. She is too busy grinning up at Chase. I swear her IQ drops fifty points whenever he's around. She tilts her head to one side. Her blond pageboy falls over one shoulder. "I'm going over to Whelan's. You want to come?" she says to him. She bites on her lower lip, which makes her look as if she's going to burst into tears if Chase says no.

Willy and Earl have come up behind him. Willy's hair is slicked back into a DA (short for *duck's ass*, which pretty much sums up Willy). It doesn't look in the least bit cool. It just looks as if he hasn't washed his hair in a year. He pulls out a comb and smooths back the sides. "Somebody mention Whelan's? I'm in." He jerks his thumb over his shoulder without turning around. "I'm starved. Pounding the crap out of niggers who don't know their place always gives me an appetite."

Earl says, "I could eat an elephant." Earl has a bad case of acne. One of the pimples on his face has exploded. Blood and pus run along his cratered cheek. He winks over at Rayanne, who rolls her eyes in disgust.

"I didn't hear anybody inviting you along," Chase tells them.

The stupid grin slides right off Willy's face.

"You going to Whelan's, Dove?" Chase asks.

I don't answer. I'm watching Gator. By now everybody is going about their business again, although they're still avoiding the other side of the street. Gator wipes the blood away from his eye with his sleeve. He presses his back against the brick wall and slowly pulls himself to his feet.

"Dove?" Chase says.

I ignore him.

Gator takes a step away from the wall. He stops—I guess to see if he'll be steady enough on his feet—then moves on down the street. Not once does he look our way. Even from over here, I can see there is blood on the sidewalk where he was sitting.

"Dove, Chase is talking to you," Rayanne says. She nudges me with her shoulder.

"Really? Well, maybe I'm not talking to him." I start to walk away. "I have to get home," I call over my shoulder to a speechless Rayanne.

Chase frowns at me like he doesn't have any idea who I am.

And right now, neither do I.

When I get home, I find Delia sitting on the top step of the back porch.
Her arms rest on her knees. One hand holds a cigarette, the
other a book. A laundry basket heaped with wet clothes sits
next to her. She's so busy reading I'm not sure she even hears
the screen door slap shut.

I slide my back down the pillar and pull my legs up to my
chest. It's been almost an hour since Willy and Earl beat up
Gator, but the trembling going on inside me hasn't let up.
Every time I close my eyes, I see blood all over the sidewalk.
I can't get that picture out of my head.

I'm mad as blazes at Chase for not trying to stop Willy
and Earl. But I'm even madder at myself. The truth is, I was

afraid of what folks might think—me sticking up for a colored man.

When Delia finally looks over at me, all she says is, "What you gone and done to your hair?"

"Got it cut."

"Well, I can *see* that." She takes a long drag from her cigarette.

I don't want to get off on some discussion about my hair. I already know it looks bad. I reach over, snatch her cigarette, knocking off the ash, and manage to take a short drag before she grabs it back and slaps my hand. "You are just lookin' to *die*, aren't you? If those cigarettes don't kill you, your daddy surely will."

"*You* should talk." I point to the cigarette in her hand.

Delia ignores me and goes back to her reading.

"Must be a real interesting book," I say.

She keeps her eyes on the page in front of her. I can tell she isn't in the mood for conversation. But that's never stopped me before. I bend over so my head comes between her and the book. The scent of Pine-Sol mixed with cigarette smoke drifts up from Delia's clothes.

"Poetry? I love poetry." I pull the book toward me so I can see the cover.

She slams the book closed so fast she almost traps my nose between the pages. "Spit it out," she says.

"What?"

"You got something on your mind and you're not going to give me a minute's peace till you tell me. You're worse than a starving mosquito with all this hovering."

I want to tell her what happened to Gator. That's why I've

come looking for her. But I don't know where to start. Instead I say, "You find out what Travis was here about this morning?"

She stares out toward the groves. "Just some trouble with a few pickers."

"What kind of trouble?"

"I don't know any more than that." Delia looks me right in the eye. She is daring me not to believe her.

I lift her book from her lap and flip through it. There is a photograph of the poet on the back of the jacket. I stop flipping pages and stare at it. It is the face of a colored man.

Delia grabs the book from my hands and sets it on her other side, safely out of my reach. "You think only white folks write poems?"

I shake my head. "Of course not." Although I have to admit I never really thought about it till now.

I look over at Delia's book and suddenly I see her, plain as day, back before she started wearing Gus's clothes. She's sitting on an upside-down empty crate in the groves. She has on a faded work dress and her hair is tied up in a scarf that is wound around her head. A bunch of the pickers' kids are sitting by her feet. Gator is perched next to her on the crate and she is showing him something from a book.

I remember the sun was setting and everybody was heading back to Travis's produce truck. Chase and I were running through the groves, playing Tarzan. Chase was grabbing branches and pretending to swing from them.

When it was almost too dark to see, Delia called me. I stepped out onto the rutted sandy road a few feet from where she was sitting with Gator. All the other kids had left for the day. But Gator was still holding the book, running his finger slowly across the lines on the page, sounding out the words.

Delia and Gus's youngest boy, Jeremiah, was in high school by then. And their other children were all grown up and off on their own. Jeremiah didn't go to our school, of course. But sometimes he stopped by to pick up his mother when he was using the family car.

Watching Delia with Gator—it was like somebody grabbing my insides and twisting the life out of them. Every night Delia read me a story before she left to go home to the colored quarters. Seeing her reading to Gator, maybe even teaching him how to read, made me so jealous I picked up a rotten orange and threw it at them. It caught Gator on the shoulder.

Delia was on me in a flash. She grabbed my arm and marched me straight home. She said if I ever did anything like that again I could pretty much count on her not being around to make my breakfast the next day. That was the scariest thing I could imagine, Delia not being in my life. And somehow she knew it.

I look out over our backyard, beyond the old oaks to where the groves begin about two hundred yards away. In my mind I can still see them, Gator and Delia, sitting side by side on that crate. I think about all the paper sacks Delia has saved for Gator over the years, about how she has watched over him in her way, and I know I have to tell her about Willy and Earl.

"Something happened after the movie this afternoon," I say.

"What movie? You been to a movie? You didn't tell me you were going to no movie." She pinches the material of my shorts between her thumb and forefinger. "You went to the movie theater wearing shorts?"

"Bermuda shorts," I remind her. "They're longer." I am hoping this will appease her. Delia has some very definite ideas about what is proper for young ladies and what isn't.

"Going to town, dressed like—like—" She sputters a few times.

I pinch Gus's coveralls, the same way she pinched my Bermuda shorts. "I don't think you're the best person to tell me how to dress," I say.

Delia looks away. I know I've hurt her.

"I'm sorry," I say. "Do you want to hear what happened after the movie or not?"

She lights another cigarette. "Suit yourself."

I tell her everything that happened from the moment I saw Gator talking to Rosemary to when I left to come home.

Delia doesn't say anything for a long time. I expect her to light into me about not helping Gator, about not trying to stop Willy and Earl. But what she says is, "That boy's gonna get himself killed one of these days."

She tosses the cigarette on the step and crushes it with Gus's sneaker. She puts her hand on the small of her back and stretches. She stands up and lifts the heavy basket of wet laundry, resting it on one hip. Her face is shiny with sweat. "How'd it make you feel, watching that?"

She narrows her eyes at me. I can almost feel them burning right into my soul. Delia has a way of digging out the truth with those eyes of hers. You don't dare lie to her when she looks at you that way.

A wave of nausea washes through me. I lower my head. "Sick," I tell her. "Sick to my stomach."

She gives me one sharp nod before heading over to the clothesline, as if to say, *Good!*

· · · · · · · · · · · · · · · · ·

Sunday morning, after Dad and I get home from church, I change into a pair of shorts, slip on my sneakers, and head for the groves to find Gator. I want to make sure he's okay after the beating he took the day before.

A soft breeze blows through the trees, filling me up with the scent of Valencia blossoms. I keep an eye out for Travis Waite. I don't need any more lectures on staying out of my own groves.

Up ahead Eli is talking to some of the pickers. Gator isn't with them. Teak and Jody are playing a few yards from me. They're swinging sticks, pretending to have a sword fight.

"Either of you seen Gator?"

Teak lets the arm holding his stick sword drop to his side. He is wearing a T-shirt that is so big, it covers his knees. I can't be sure if he is even wearing shorts underneath it. He cups a hand above his eyes like a visor and stares up at me. "Gator ain't been around since yesterday morning," he tells me.

Jody is practicing his own version of sword-fighting footwork. He bounces back and forth on the balls of his feet like a prizefighter, swinging his stick. "Saw him at the camp," he says.

He is talking about the migrant camp where all the pickers stay. "When?"

"Last night." Jody whips the stick in the air, hard and fast. It makes threatening zipping sounds.

"He's okay, then?"

Jody stops his footwork. He and Teak give each other a look.

I wait.

Teak chews on his lower lip.

"Well? Is he?"

Jody spins around on one foot, holding his stick sword with both hands above his head. I get this unsettling feeling that when he stops spinning he is going to lunge right at me.

"Sure," Teak says. He springs forward, launching his stick at Jody, who laughs and jumps back. I've been rescued.

The two of them chase each other, kicking sand onto my sneakers as they take off to find the other pickers. The others have moved on. They are out of my line of vision.

I stand in one of the ruts in the sandy dirt road. I have no idea where to find Gator.

The sun is directly overhead now. Blazing hot. The breeze is gone. Everything is still. Only muffled voices—the shouts of the pickers calling to each other—fill the space around me. But I don't see anyone.

I step off the road into a line of trees. When I was a kid, I used to think nothing of climbing up through those branches and pulling an orange from the top. That's where the oranges are the sweetest. I shade my eyes and look up. The branches are too dense to climb. I'll end up with scratches all over my arms and legs. Instead I settle for an orange from the south side that I can reach.

I crawl under the lower branches to find shade. It's cool under here, like being beneath a dark green umbrella. Chase and Gator and I used to hide under these trees all the time when we were playing. They were our caves, our forts, our private sanctuaries.

The branches are weighted down with oranges. They are so low that I can lean only my shoulders against the tree trunk. With my thumb I dig a hole in the orange, tear away part of the peel, and bite into the fruit. I squeeze the sweet juice into my mouth. It runs down my arm; it dribbles off my chin, making orange splotches on my blouse. The sand beneath me is smooth, cool, and weedless. My eyes are heavy. Before I realize it, I've fallen asleep.

The sound of angry voices rips me awake. It takes me a few seconds to remember where I am.

The pickers must be working in the area. I pull back a few branches and look. No one is there. But the muffled, agitated voices are nearby. I crawl over to the other side of the tree. The voices are closer over here, although I can't make out what they are saying. They are speaking in Spanish.

I part a small space in the leaves. Two young men, Mexicans, stand barely twenty feet away. They wear dusty dungarees, sweaty T-shirts, and what look like cowboy hats, only made of straw. One is short and barrel-shaped. The other has a thick mustache and seems to be a few years older. The barrel-shaped man flings his arms upward and shakes them in short, sharp jerks, as if he is holding an invisible watermelon he is about to dash to the ground.

The mustache man puts a hand on the barrel man's shoulder. His voice is softer. I can tell by his tone that he is trying to reason with the other man. *"Si hace eso ahí será el diablo,"* he says. *"El* diablo, *amigo."*

The barrel man stops waving his arms and looks away.

"¿Me oyes?" says the other.

The barrel man lowers his head and rubs his eyes with his thumb and forefinger. *"Pero mi niño. ¡Mi hijo!"* This last comes out like a sob. I feel it rumble in my own chest.

I recognize one word. *Niño. Baby.* The other man keeps his hand on the barrel man's shoulder. He leans toward him and speaks in a reassuring tone. The barrel man shakes his head, keeping it down.

The men turn to leave. I crawl out from under the tree just as a shadow darkens the ground in front of me and find myself looking right into Gator's bruised and swollen face.

"Is this what you do in the groves now?" he asks.

I stand up and brush the dirt off me. "I was cooling off." I don't bother to mention I was taking a nap.

Gator stares at me as if he isn't sure I'm telling the truth. Above his left eye is a red, puckered gash. A bruise smudges his left cheek. He is wearing his faded red T-shirt again. I can't help but wonder about the blue shirt, the new one. Was he able to wash the bloodstains from it?

"We used to play under these trees all the time when we were kids. To get out of the sun, remember?" I don't know why I feel I need to remind him of this. But I do.

"Looks to me like the games have changed," he says.

When I don't answer—because I'm not sure what he's

getting at—he jerks his chin in the direction of the two Mexicans. The mustache man has his hand pressed against the barrel man's spine, as if to keep him from falling backward.

I turn to Gator. "I wasn't eavesdropping if that's what you're thinking." With a sickening feeling I realize that maybe Gator thinks I've been spying on the pickers for my dad.

"Gator, they were speaking Spanish. I don't even know what they were talking about, for heaven's sake. I don't know any Spanish."

He studies me with those eyes of his, eyes the color of raisins. Then he raises his hand and points at the backs of the two men. "They were talking about the camp store."

"There's a store at the migrant camp?" I've never been to the camp. For all I know it's like a town, complete with shops and a main street.

He nods.

"I thought they were talking about a baby."

Gator gets this twitch of a smile in one corner of his mouth. "I thought you didn't speak Spanish."

"Well, I don't, Gator. I recognized that word is all. From playing in the groves, I guess."

Gator kicks at the sand with a bare foot. Sand flies every which way. "That's Julio Gonzalez. He's got a new son."

"Oh." I wait to see if he's going to say more. When he doesn't, I ask, "What's that got to do with the camp store?"

Gator stares up at one of the trees. I can tell he's trying to decide whether or not to answer that question. "I'd better let Eli know the fruit's getting too ripe on those top branches," he says.

He turns to leave.

"I'm sorry," I tell him. I point to the gash on his forehead.

He gives me a curt nod before he heads down the road, a nod that puts me in mind of the one Delia gave me the day before, after I told her about Willy and Earl and about how what they did to Gator made me sick to my stomach.

Delia is whipping up a batch of her cracklin' corn bread when I come through the back door. She's got a ham baking in the oven. I head straight for the stairs. I have a ton of homework to do. That's the worst thing about Sunday afternoons.

"Just you hold on there," Delia says, wiping her hands on an old dishtowel she has tucked in the waistband of Gus's patched khaki trousers. "Not so fast."

I stop in the doorway that leads into the hall. By the tone of her voice I know I'm in trouble.

She reaches into the cabinet next to the sink and pulls out a Campbell's soup can.

I stare down at the red-and-white label, wondering if

Delia is planning to make soup to go with our Sunday dinner. But when she bangs the can on the counter and I hear the hollow sound, I know what's coming. With Delia, it's always better to face the storm head-on rather than stand still and wait for a bolt of lightning to take you down.

"You've been going through my personal things!" I'm not really all that upset about this. Delia more than likely found the soup can by accident while she was cleaning. She isn't the snooping type. But I have to make it seem as if Delia is the one who's done something wrong if I'm going to win this round.

Delia holds out the soup can with her thumb and forefinger, waving it under my nose. "And *you* been smoking behind my back."

I don't have to look to know there are six or seven smelly cigarette butts squashed in the bottom of the can. "You have no business rooting through my closet."

"Well, then, I expect you can bring your own dirty clothes down to the laundry room from now on." Delia slams the soup can on the table. "You think I couldn't smell those old butts the minute I opened your closet door? They were just asking to be found."

"It's none of your business what I do."

Delia picks up the wooden spoon and begins beating the corn bread batter within an inch of its life. She doesn't say anything, and that makes me nervous.

"You going to tell Dad?"

"He's going to want to know his baby's trying to kill herself."

I head for the refrigerator and stand in front of the open

door, stalling for time, trying to think what I can do to keep Delia from telling my dad. Most of the time, if I play my cards right, Delia and I can reach some kind of compromise. It's all a matter of finding the right thing to barter with.

"You planning to refrigerate the whole kitchen?" Delia snaps. She bends down to lift the glazed ham from the oven and sets it on top of the stove.

I pretend I don't hear her and go right on taking stock of my choices, finally deciding on the Hawaiian Punch.

Delia pours the corn bread batter into the greased cast-iron skillet, scraping the bowl with a rubber spatula. She slides the pan into the oven.

I pour myself a glass of punch and sit down at the table.

"You want something to eat with that?" She points to my glass.

"No thanks."

One thing I'll say for Delia. No matter how mad she gets at me, it never stops her from making sure I've got a full belly.

Delia slides out a chair and sits down, not saying anything, just watching. Then she pulls a box of Vicks cough drops from the pocket of Gus's trousers. "This is what you get smoking. You get a cough that feels like it's going to take your whole insides along with it on its way up and turn you clear inside out." She slides a cough drop from the box and pops it into her mouth.

I lift the soup can and shake it, listening to the dull rattle of the cigarette butts inside. Somehow I can't muster up the energy to get all that upset over Delia's discovery. Even if she does tell my dad, the worst that will probably happen is that I'll get grounded for a week or two.

Delia leans back in the chair, arms folded, watching me. She's waiting to see what I've got to say about those cigarette butts.

I take a long swallow of punch. "Is something going on with the pickers?"

Not one single muscle in Delia's face moves. "Now just how would I know that?"

With my finger I sketch a stick figure in the sweat on my glass. "Because you know most of them. I was wondering . . ." I want to ask her the question I should have asked Gator when we were talking in the groves, except I got so rattled when he thought I was spying on the pickers, I forgot.

"Well, spit it out."

"Are they having some kind of trouble over at the camp store?"

"Who?"

"The pickers, for heaven's sake. We're talking about the pickers, remember?"

"Don't want any of your sassin'." She waves a warning finger in my face. "I don't know anything about that ol' migrant camp, so you can just save those questions for somebody else."

Delia isn't being honest with me. I can feel it. She knows something and she's not going to tell me.

She pulls the dishtowel from the waistband of Gus's trousers and tosses it on the table.

"How come you always wear Gus's old clothes?" I ask. I know darn good and well that Delia doesn't like being reminded about what happened to Gus. But I'm upset with her for saying she doesn't know anything about what's going on with the pickers when I know she does.

Delia folds her arms tight across her chest. "Now why you asking me that?"

"I don't know. Just wondering is all."

Delia doesn't say anything right away. She's trying to figure out if I'm up to something. Finally she says, "Well, then, I got my reasons—not that they're any of your business."

"What kind of reasons?"

"Well, for one thing, I like wearing his clothes because it's like having a part of him still with me. You know what I'm saying?" She tilts her head back and thrusts her chin at me. "Now if you want to call me crazy, you go right on and do it."

I get up to pour another glass of punch. I was only two weeks away from my fourth birthday when my mom died. I don't remember her face at all, only the smell of her clothes. "I don't think you're crazy," I tell Delia.

I close the fridge door and look over at her. "After Mom died, I used to sneak into her closet, close the door, and bury my face in her dresses, breathing in the scent of her powder and bath soap. I used to sit on the floor for hours with my eyes closed, pretending she was right there in the closet with me. Then Dad gave all her clothes to the Salvation Army, and I didn't know where to go to be with Mom after that. But as long as her clothes were there, it was like she was still here with me."

I come back to the table and sit down.

Delia nods and I know she understands. "I got this old sweater of Gus's. I don't wear it or anything. I keep it folded up nice in my dresser drawer. Except sometimes I take it out and hold it on my lap if I'm having a bad day.

"I haven't washed that sweater since the night my Gus

died. Can't seem to bring myself to do it. It smells just like him. A little bit of that Old Spice he'd splash on himself after shaving, a little bit of those cigars he smoked when we could afford 'em, a dab of that pomade he slicked his hair back with—all those smells, and something of his own, too, that didn't get splashed on or smeared on, something that came right from his skin.

"He had that sweater with him the night he died, but he wasn't wearing it. He'd tied the sleeves around his saxophone case and was carrying it with him. If he'd been wearing it, it would of got all tore up, soaked in blood more than likely."

I knew Gus had been killed in a hit-and-run. But I never knew how it happened. I'm not sure Delia will tell me, but I ask her anyway.

"You don't want to hear that, child."

"Yes I do."

Delia watches me for a few minutes, not saying anything. Then she gets up to check the corn bread. "Not today, sugar." She has her back to me.

"Please."

"Someday, maybe. Just not today." Her voice is soft and smooth as pudding and sounds far away.

There's no wheedling anything out of Delia if she isn't in the mood to talk. I finally give in and head upstairs.

Our house has two stories. My great-granddaddy Alderman wanted it that way, a big white house with a porch across the front and a smaller back porch. Most of the houses around here are only one story, except the Tully place and a few others.

My curtains balloon, catching the soft breeze coming

through my windows. I close my eyes and breathe. The air is so heavy with the scent of orange blossoms from our groves that it makes me a little light-headed.

I kick off my sneakers and flop down on the pink flowered bedspread that Delia helped me pick out of the Sears Roebuck catalog a few months back. We picked out matching curtains too, since my dad doesn't know the first thing about decorating a girl's room.

Thinking back over those years after my mom died, the face I remember best is Delia's. She has always been here. Spraying Bactine on my scraped knees, baking my birthday cakes every year, buying me my first sanitary napkins and a belt, and then explaining how to use them, washing my hair with foul-smelling medicine when the whole third grade thought they'd caught head lice from the Dobbin twins—which turned out not to be the case, but it upset a lot of folks just the same.

It was Delia who gave me my name. I was three weeks old, and Mom and Dad still couldn't agree on whether to name me after my great-grandma Tilly—Mom's grandmother—or my dad's aunt Nora. Up till then, everybody called me Sugar Baby. Then one morning Delia was rocking me back and forth in my carriage on the front porch when this ringed turtledove landed right on my belly. It had soft beige-white feathers and a black ring across the back of its neck, like a tiny kerchief. It sat there on my blanket for the longest while, cocking its head to one side, then the other, like it was contemplating something. At least that's how Delia tells it.

She told my mom and dad that she was purely certain that turtledove was a sign from heaven. The Lord figured I'd gone on long enough without a name and decided to give me one himself. I'm just glad Delia didn't think the Lord was trying to name me Turtle.

Delia's hugs have always been mixed up in my mind with the scent of Vicks cough drops, lemon furniture polish, and the musty smell of cigarette smoke that clings to her clothes. This mixture of scents has sealed Delia's hugs in my mind forever. I cannot smell Vicks cough drops without feeling warm and safe. Sometimes I even buy a box at the drugstore just to smell them.

And here, all this time, Delia has had a whole other life apart from Dad and me. She has had Gus and Jeremiah and her other children. A life I've never really paid much attention to before. Maybe because I didn't like sharing her with anybody else. I wanted her there just for me. When Gus died and Jeremiah went off to college, I finally did have her all to myself, except for her taking care of my dad, of course.

Until now, when Delia left to go home each night, I no more thought about where she was going than I wondered where the stars went each morning. I just expected them to come back. Like Delia did each day. If that ever changed, I expect my whole world would come crashing down.

8

For two agonizing hours I have been working on an essay about Emily Dickinson's poem, number 744, for Miss Poyer's class, and wondering why all Emily Dickinson's poems are numbered. Couldn't she think up titles, for heaven's sake?

I love reading poems out loud, the sound of the words, the rhythms. But I don't much like writing essays about them. So far all I have are three stupid paragraphs that more or less say the same thing three different ways. Miss Poyer doesn't let us get away with this sort of thing. She calls it writing in circles, and she's always on the lookout for it.

The reason I have chosen this poem is because it is about remorse. It begins "Remorse—is Memory—awake—." I've been feeling a little of that remorse myself lately, after what happened to Gator the day before. So I was curious to see what Emily Dickinson had to say on the subject. Only, trying to understand one of her poems is like trying to break some sort of Soviet spy code.

I slouch in my chair and tap the end of my pencil on my desk. I pick up another pencil and rap them both, playing the top of my desk like a drum. I'm giving serious thought to changing my topic to the excessive use of dashes in the poems of Emily Dickinson.

My desk sits right in front of my window. The wind has suddenly kicked up its heels and it's whipping the Spanish moss into a frenzy. It's dark out, so until now there hasn't been much to distract me except for the distant rumble of thunder.

Then, *zap!* Lightning zigzags toward the ground and for a panicky moment I think it might have hit someplace in the groves. My ears are cocked toward the open window, listening for a loud crack, but when it doesn't come, I relax.

It's still dry as toast out there. We've had only one tiny sneeze of a storm since Friday afternoon when Chase gave me a ride home from the cemetery. It lasted barely five minutes. Nothing that would help with this drought.

I try not to think about Chase. Whenever I do, I think of Gator getting the tar beat out of him. And Chase and I just standing there, doing nothing.

I go back to reading Emily Dickinson's poem.

Remorse is cureless—the Disease
Not even God—can heal—

For 'tis His institution—and
The Adequate of Hell—

I am staring at that last line, with my eyes practically burning a hole in the page, when a loud roar of thunder rattles the windows in my room. The blast that follows is louder than any shotgun I've ever heard. More like an explosion. I nearly jump out of my chair.

The flash of lightning, streaking down the side of our barn, is so bright it hurts my eyes. The next thing I know, flames are leaping into the air.

I charge downstairs, two at a time, and out the back door. Flames are licking away at the boards of our barn. My first thought is to grab the hose by the house. But before I reach it, I hear the back door slam. My dad is coming right at me, carrying a fire extinguisher like he's cradling a newborn.

"Call the fire department!" he yells as he runs past me.

Somehow I make it back to the house, even though my legs have gone all rubbery. It feels as if my bones are dissolving.

The phone numbers of the police and fire departments are on the bulletin board beside the phone in the kitchen. I squint at them, but they're just a blur. I can't seem to focus my eyes. My hands are shaking so badly I can hardly dial. Desperate, I dial 0 for the local operator, give her our address, and tell her what is happening.

By the time I get back one whole side of our barn is in flames. A fifty-year-old barn, built by my great-granddaddy Alderman, going up like a tinderbox.

The night sky flames orange as if every star is being burned out of the heavens. Even the Spanish moss waving in the trees seems to glow. The smoke stings my eyes and burns my throat. Chunks of burning ash disappear into the dark sky. I am terrified they will set the moss on fire on their journey skyward, turning our oak trees into flaming torches.

With all this thunder and lightning crashing around, you'd think there would be some rain. But so far, not a single drop. If ever we needed a downpour, it's right this very minute, before the fire swallows up everything in sight.

Through the smoke I see Dad soaking down the side of the barn with the garden hose. I pick up the fire extinguisher lying on the ground nearby, but it's already empty.

That's when I realize someone else is here, standing a few feet away, beating at the flames with something.

I drop the empty fire extinguisher, take a step back, and stare right into Chase Tully's sooty face. He stops pounding the flames and stands frozen, holding his singed leather jacket like a dead animal. He looks as if he can't believe this is happening.

I don't have time to think about what Chase is doing here. My dad is shouting, "It's too late. I got to get those tractors out!" He runs inside the barn. Chase follows, but Dad won't let him go in.

An engine roars and here comes Dad on one of the tractors. He parks it in the field across the way. Most of my dad's equipment—his new tractor, the smudge pots, kerosene, fertilizer, and all—are stored in the new barn Dad had built two years ago. It's metal. Good thing too. No telling what would have happened if the kerosene and fertilizer were in the old barn. We'd probably all be blown to smithereens.

My dad heads back to the barn to get the other tractor.

"Dad! Don't!" I shout. "The gasoline in the tractor—it

could catch fire and explode!" I am scared out of my wits he will try to save that tractor anyway. But he stops a few feet from the door. His mouth hangs open as he watches the flames swallow up what is left inside.

I stand next to him, tears streaming down my face. It isn't only a barn we're losing, it's a piece of Alderman history. That's what has to be going through his mind too. "It was lightning," I tell him. "Did you see it hit?"

"Can't say as I did." He shakes his head. "I been meaning to put that lightning rod up. It's been sitting in the barn now for two years." He wipes the sweat from his face with the sleeve of his T-shirt. "Damn it to hell." He all but spits the words out.

I can tell by the look on his face that he's going to blame himself for this fire till the day he dies. And there isn't a whole lot I can say to change his mind. If he had put up that lightning rod, maybe we wouldn't be standing here, watching our barn collapse into a heap of ashes. I feel bad for him.

The scream of sirens whistles through the night. Two fire trucks from Benevolence tear up the dirt road by our house and park a safe distance from what is left of the barn. A second squad of fire trucks arrives from nearby Brighton, followed by Moss Henley and Jimmy Wheeler in their police cruisers.

Moss comes lumbering across the yard. Those bulldog shoulders of his shift one way then the other. His thumbs are hooked in his belt, the one that holds his holster and gun. Jimmy follows behind him. Jimmy isn't wearing his police hat. His crew cut puts me in mind of a fresh-mowed lawn.

"Spudder's on his way," Moss tells my dad. Spudder Rhodes is the chief of police. Spudder, Moss, and Jimmy make up the entire Benevolence police force.

By now the gas in the tractor has caught fire. The explosion roars into the night. A ball of flame shoots through the place where the barn roof used to be.

Men pull hoses from the fire trucks and charge headlong toward the flames. But it's too late. Anybody can see that just by looking at the pile of glowing cinders in our yard. Still, they keep the water coming till there isn't a single burning ember left. Nothing but the stink of wet, charred wood. They don't want to take any chances that the fire might smolder. If the dry grass starts burning again, the fire could spread to the house. The firefighters even soak down the nearby oaks and Spanish moss.

We stand there, Dad, Chase, and I, watching the men do their job and feeling about as useful as three lawn mowers in a snowstorm. Dad circles my shoulders with his arm and pulls me close.

The firemen are packing up their equipment and getting ready to head out when Spudder Rhodes finally shows up. He isn't wearing his police uniform. Just khakis and a striped polo shirt. He moseys on up to my dad, belly tumbling over his belt, like he's just out for an evening stroll and happened by. My dad tells Chase and me to head on back to the house. He needs to talk to Spudder.

• • • • • • • • • • • • • • • • •

Chase and I are leaning over the kitchen sink, scrubbing the soot off our hands and faces, when my dad comes through the door. He looks like a whipped pup.

I hand Chase a towel. His hands aren't burned, at least

not much. The hair is singed in a few places, and there is one nasty blister in the spot between his thumb and forefinger. But that's about it.

He's watching me with this little smirk on his face, which is when it dawns on me that I'm standing here in my grodiest dungarees and one of my dad's old T-shirts, with my hair in rollers. Any other time I would have made a beeline for my bedroom and not come out again till I resembled a human being. But our barn has just burned to the ground, and I don't much care how I look.

"You see the lightning hit?" Dad asks Chase.

Chase shakes his head. He circles his face with the towel a few times. "No. I was driving past your house when I saw the fire. When I got here, I heard you telling Dove to call the fire department. Then I just started beating the flames."

Dad puts his hand on Chase's shoulder and eases him into a chair. Then he looks straight at me. "How about you make us some coffee, Dove. And see about getting some salve and bandages for Chase's hand."

Chase's hand isn't that bad, so I take longer than I need to, making the coffee. I have to go upstairs to the medicine cabinet for the bandages, and I don't want to miss anything.

"It caught the edge of the barn roof and skidded right down the side," I tell them. Dad hasn't even bothered to ask me about it. "The lightning, Dad. You were asking Chase if he saw it hit."

Dad stands there, his eyes aimed on me while I make coffee. He doesn't say anything. I don't fault him for not paying any attention to what I'm telling him, even though it bothers me a little. I can tell his mind is someplace else. Finally he wanders over to the refrigerator and gets himself a bottle of beer. He digs around in one of the kitchen drawers for a bottle opener.

After a few swallows, he comes up behind Chase and pats him on the shoulder. "I'm glad you were here, son."

He looks over at me. "Dove, you planning to get those bandages anytime before Christmas?"

It's on the tip of my tongue to remind him that I was there too and wasn't he glad about that? But I don't say anything. I head upstairs, grab what I need, and hurry back to the kitchen.

Dad tells me to take care of Chase's hand, then goes off to finish talking to Spudder, who is still outside looking around. I don't know what Spudder thinks he'll find. Lightning's lightning. It doesn't hang around for questioning.

The whole time I'm bandaging Chase's hand, he's staring at me with that little smile twitching on his lips, like he finds it funny, my being his nurse. And wouldn't you know, right when I'm thinking this, he says, "You'd make a fine nurse, Dove."

Suddenly my mind skitters back to when I was six years old and the two of us were hidden up in the loft of our barn— the one that just burned down—playing what seemed at the time to be a particularly interesting game of nurse and doctor. Chase is probably the only person outside of my family, with the exception of Doc Martindale, to have seen parts of my body that no one has any business seeing.

I focus my attention on fixing his hand. I can't bring myself to look at him.

"You got a real soft touch," he says, resting his free hand on top of mine.

Goose bumps are doing the jitterbug all up and down my arm. There's no way to hide something like that.

Chase looks down at my arm and smiles.

"How come you didn't help Gator yesterday?" I ask, slipping my hand out of his.

"Whoa! Where'd that come from?"

"Willy and Earl were beating the tar out of him. You could have stopped it."

"Maybe. Maybe not." Chase stares down at his bandaged hand. "You weren't exactly charging across the street yelling for time-outs either, you know."

He's right about that. I honestly don't have any business asking him about what he did or didn't do. Not when I stood there, doing nothing but watching, like everybody else.

"I know," I say. "And I get angry at myself every time I think about it."

Chase nods like he understands. "It's just the way it is, Dove."

"Why? Why does it have to be that way?"

He shakes his head. Chase doesn't know the answer to this one any more than I do.

I get up to pour us some coffee just as my dad comes through the door. Jacob Tully is with him. He must have seen the fire from his place and come to help.

Dad stares down at Chase's bandage. "How's your hand, son? You want me to take you to the emergency room?"

"Doc Alderman here fixed me up just fine." Chase grins at me.

Jacob Tully stands there digging his finger in one ear. He is almost a full head taller than my dad, thin, but broad in the shoulders. His thick hair is streaked with white. He has on a pair of khakis and a light blue shirt.

Chase's dad has this long face with deep gouges running on either side of his nose down to his chin. He looks almost angry. But then, for long as I can remember, Jacob Tully has never looked any other way.

"Spudder says he'd appreciate any information you can give Moss and Jimmy for their report," Jacob tells Chase.

Chase doesn't so much as glance his dad's way. His hands are in front of him on the kitchen table. He's got his eyes glued on those hands.

The look on Jacob Tully's face makes me think he's about to lunge across the room and grab Chase by the shoulder to get his attention. But right about then my dad says, "It's almost eleven o'clock." He points to the clock above the sink. "You probably got homework to do."

Chase nods, somehow managing to keep a straight face. As far as I know, he hasn't opened a book since fifth grade. But he always seems to get by.

Dad walks Chase to the door and thanks him again.

Jacob nods our way as he turns to leave, but doesn't say another word. Seems like he's got something weighing on his mind too.

After Chase leaves, I pour my dad a cup of coffee and sit across from him at the table. It about breaks my heart losing our barn. But we still have a roof over our heads. And Dad and I still have each other.

Word about our barn spreads almost as fast as the flames had. At school I have a swarm of kids buzzing around me in the hall, wanting to know about the fire. I am practically a celebrity. I tell them every little detail, including how Chase tried to beat out the flames with his jacket.

Rayanne's tweezed eyebrows shoot clear up to her scalp. "You mean the black leather one?"

Everybody in Benevolence knows how important that jacket is to Chase. Beating out the flames with it to save our barn is the ultimate sacrifice.

Rayanne frowns. "It's the middle of April, for heaven's sake. Is he still wearing that thing?"

"Yeah, he is. And he'd like 'that thing' back." It is Chase himself.

The kids part like the Red Sea, letting him through just as the bell rings for homeroom.

I run to my locker to get my books. Chase is right behind me. "I meant it about my jacket."

I shrug. "I'll bring it tomorrow. It's still on the back porch. What's left of it, anyway." The words are barely out of my mouth before I start to feel guilty. Chase really loves that jacket. "My dad'll get you a new one," I tell him.

"Nah, he doesn't have to do that. I'll wear my old one. It'll look broke in, like it's seen real action."

I nod a few times, not sure what to say, then grab my books and head off to homeroom. Chase stays right by my side. He walks me all the way to the door, then stands there while I go in and take my seat. I don't quite know what to make of that, seeing as how he's never done this before.

Rayanne is filing her nails. I slide into my seat across from her.

The hand holding the nail file pauses in midair. "What's with you and Chase?" Rayanne has this little blue scarf tied around her ponytail that matches her blue blouse and pleated blue-plaid skirt. Everything perfectly color coordinated. For some reason that gets on my nerves today.

"Nothing," I tell her.

"Doesn't look like 'nothing' to me." She tosses the nail file into her purse and pulls out her compact to check her lipstick. "I don't know what your problem is. If Chase Tully was after me the way he's been after you lately, I'd fall right down at his feet and wait for him to carry me off."

"Well, fine. *You* go out with him, then."

Rayanne snaps her compact shut. "You're joking, right?" She frowns at me, then slumps down in her seat. "Who am I kidding? Chase would never be interested in me. You're the only person he cares about. Everybody in this school knows that."

My heart does a little flip when she says this.

"So, did they catch who did it?" Rayanne asks out of the blue.

At first I'm not sure what she is talking about. "Did what?"

"Well, set your barn on fire, for heaven's sake."

I stare at her. "Nobody set our barn on fire," I say. "It was lightning."

Rayanne stares right back at me. "Well that's not what everybody else is saying. According to Willy Podd, Chase saw some colored person taking off for the groves right about the time he drove up to your house."

"Since when do you listen to anything Willy says?"

Rayanne shrugs. "Well, it's not just him. It's like I said, everybody's talking about it." She takes a piece of Bazooka bubble gum from her purse, unwraps it, and pops it into her mouth. "It makes sense, don't you think? Considering all the fires we've had around here lately."

"It doesn't make sense at all," I say. "And for your information, I *saw* the lightning strike our barn. Nobody set it on fire."

Rayanne snaps her gum a few times. She looks as if

she's about to say something, but then Mrs. Hatch starts taking attendance. After her name is called, Rayanne leans over and whispers, "Why don't you just ask Chase for yourself?"

* * * * * * * * * * * * * * * * *

Later, on my way to the cafeteria, I catch up with Chase in front of his locker. "Have you been going around telling folks you saw somebody set fire to our barn last night?"

Chase jams a book into his locker, closing the door fast before a ton of junk comes tumbling out and buries us alive. He doesn't seem all that surprised by my question. He takes a step closer. My back is flat up against somebody's locker. I feel the heat from Chase's body. I press the palm of one hand on the metal behind me to remind myself of what something cool feels like.

"Don't tell me you've been listening to those rumors too," he says.

"Somebody had to start them," I say.

He leans forward, putting both hands on the locker, one on each side above my head, to balance his weight. His face is only inches from mine. I smell his Doublemint gum. His ice blue eyes send a little shiver through me, and my heart does a drumroll. "It wasn't me," he says.

"Who, then?" My voice sounds wobbly. Not at all like me. I can't stop looking at his mouth. It's only a few inches from my own. My body tips toward him. I have no idea where Rayanne got the idea that Chase likes me, but for once in my life I'm hoping she's right about something. I'm pondering this interesting new development when the bell rings, and I realize I've made Chase late for class.

"Later," he says. Then he is gone, heading down the hall with his slow, easy strut. From the back, he sort of reminds me of Gator.

* * * * * * * * * * * * * * * *

I make a dash for the cafeteria. We get only twenty minutes for lunch. Half of that time we spend in line. I'm almost to the door when I hear somebody say, "You're Dove Alderman, right?"

I look over to see Rosemary, the girl from Luellen's, coming up beside me. I'm wondering how she found out my name. From Luellen or Nona, maybe.

Kids bump past us on their rush to the food troughs. I step away from the doorway, not sure what Rosemary is doing here.

"I heard about your barn," she says. "I'm real sorry. It was an accident, right?"

"Lightning," I tell her.

Rosemary takes a deep breath, as if she's relieved to hear this. She stands there, picking at the frayed corner of her three-ring binder. "I'm Rosemary Howell. Luellen's cousin." She pulls at a loose thread and the corner of the binder unravels a little bit more.

"Uh-huh. . . ." I wait to see if there's more information coming. There is.

"I just started school here a few weeks ago."

I nod. Rosemary makes me nervous. No, it's more than that. She makes me feel guilty. I don't much like being re-minded of last Saturday, me being one of the gawking crowd and all, and not lifting a finger to stop what was going on. I'm waiting for her to point this out to me, but all she says is, "I'm a junior."

"Well, that's real nice," I say, inching my way toward the cafeteria. I'm hoping she'll take the hint.

Rosemary is right behind me as I head through the open doors. "Is this your lunch period?" she asks.

Since I am now standing in line—the very *end* of the line—I don't feel I have to answer this.

"Mine too," she says, even though I haven't said any-thing.

"When did you start working for Luellen?" I ask, trying to be polite.

"Well . . ." She gives this question far more thought than it deserves. "It's been about five weeks, I guess."

"Are you staying with her?" Everybody in town knows Luellen lives in the apartment above her beauty shop.

"Sort of." Rosemary looks away. Her fingers are still working on that frayed corner. If she's not careful, the whole cloth cover is going to unravel.

"Sort of?"

"I mean, it's just for now."

I notice she's wearing saddle shoes that are so scuffed and dirty, I doubt they've ever been polished. Her dress is a faded plaid and the lace around her Peter Pan collar is hanging loose in two places. If it's true what Erdine Tucker said, that Rosemary's folks are pickers, I can't help but wonder why she's staying at Luellen's and not with her family. But I don't ask.

We slide our trays along the metal bars. I take the turkey and mashed potatoes platter. Rosemary just keeps shoving her tray along until we get to the desserts. She takes a small square of spice cake. I pay my fifty cents and head off to meet Rayanne and our other friends.

Rayanne glares at me when I set my tray down.

"What?" I glare back at her.

She's looking past me. I don't have to turn around to know who she's staring at. Rosemary comes up beside me with her little square of spice cake in one corner of her tray. The frayed notebook fills the rest of the space.

There's not a whole lot a person can do in a situation like this. So I pretend that her joining us has been my idea all along. "Uh . . . everybody," I say. "This is Rosemary Howell. She, um . . . just started going to school here a few weeks back."

Rayanne is looking at me as if I just shot her dog. The others shift their eyes from me, to Rosemary, to each other. Except for Jinny Culpepper, who is nice to everybody. Jinny's charm bracelet jangles as she gives Rosemary a little wave. "Hey, Rosemary," she says.

"She's a junior," I tell them. I am hoping this will impress them enough to let Rosemary sit at our table. It never hurts to have an upperclassman eating lunch with you.

Unfortunately no one is the least bit impressed. I point to the empty seat next to mine. "You can sit here if you want," I tell Rosemary.

The relief in her smile only makes me feel worse.

Everyone goes back to talking. Just not to Rosemary. I shovel food in my mouth at the rate of a forkful per second. We have only three minutes before the bell and my next class. Rayanne is sending me hate messages with her eyes.

I am so busy concentrating on swallowing without choking that I don't see Willy and Earl coming across the room until they are right at the end of our table.

"Well if it ain't our little nigger lover," Willy says. He raps his knuckles on the table a few times. It's as if somebody bumped the arm on a record player—first there's this sharp scrape, then total silence. Everybody at our table has stopped talking. Their eyes are on Willy and Earl.

Rosemary hasn't touched her cake, although she has her fork in her hand and seems to be working up to the part where she actually puts it in the food. Now she lays the fork carefully beside the plate. She stares down at the cake. Her eyes are glued to that white frosting.

"Drop dead, Willy," I say.

He snickers over his shoulder at Earl. "Looks like we got us another one."

The only sound I hear, besides the one coming from Willy's big mouth, is the clanking of dishes and silverware from the kitchen. I never noticed before how much racket the kitchen help makes back there.

"Maybe we got us a whole table full," Willy says.

Rayanne is on her feet so fast she has to grab the back of her chair for balance. She lifts her tray and holds it close to her, as if she's afraid they might try to snatch it from her.

"Jerks!" she mutters, and heads over to the window to drop off the tray.

"Whoo-eee! The chick's frosted." Willy laughs and shakes his hand hard and fast.

Just then the bell rings and everybody jumps up from their seats at the same time. The moment is so synchronized, you'd have thought they'd rehearsed it.

"Come on," I say to Rosemary. I am not about to leave her here with Willy and Earl. Rosemary lifts her notebook and gets up, forgetting her tray, and heads straight for the door. I dump my tray at the window and take off after her.

"They're complete morons," I tell her when I finally catch up. "Together their IQs don't even add up to a hundred."

Rosemary is moving down the hall at record speed, shoving her way past guys on the football team who are twice her size. Too bad we don't have a women's track team. We'd be state champs for sure.

Rosemary screeches to a halt in front of the chemistry lab door. I can't help her from here on. I'm supposed to be in French in less than a minute. But I don't want to leave her.

"The bell's going to ring any second," she warns. "You're gonna be late." She peeks inside the classroom door and checks out the room. Then she turns back to me. "It's okay. I can take care of myself."

I have serious doubts about this. A picture of Earl grabbing her by the wrist and yanking her away from Gator pops into my head. It gives me the creeps.

Rosemary slips into the classroom and sits on one of the

stools. Before I can turn away, Willy Podd all but knocks me off my feet as he lunges through the door. He takes a seat way in the back of the classroom. He and Earl are both juniors, like Rosemary. The odds are definitely not in Rosemary's favor.

10

"Who is she, anyway? Somebody said she's one of the pickers."
Rayanne is puffing along like a steam engine, trying to keep
up with me on our way to Whelan's after school. Whelan's is
at the other end of Main Street, clear on the opposite side of
town from the high school. I want to get there and leave before it's mobbed with kids. Seniors, mostly. Very popular seniors. They pretty much take over the place after three o'clock.

Chase wasn't around after last period, and his car was
gone from the parking lot. I'm almost positive I'll find him at
Whelan's. I want to know how those stupid rumors about our
barn got started and why he didn't try to stop them.

"Her *parents* are pickers," I tell Rayanne. I see Erdine

Tucker's face leaning into mine, whispering to me about Rosemary. "Actually, that's just something I heard. Maybe it isn't even true."

"Well, then? So she *is* a picker. Her folks are, anyway."

"Are you listening to me, Rayanne? I said I'm not even sure it's true. She's here, isn't she? She's in school like the rest of us. She is not up on a ladder in the groves. She is not hunched over a row of bush beans."

Rayanne starts chewing on her lower lip. "You shouldn't have asked her to sit with us."

"Why not?" I already know the answer to this. I just want to make her say it.

"Well, Dove, for heaven's sake, you know why."

"Why?"

Rayanne starts working on that lower lip again. Chewing like there's no tomorrow. "You heard what Willy called her."

"Since when do you side with the likes of Willy Podd?"

"I'm not! But you've got to think of our reputations. She's a migrant worker—or her folks are, anyway. And she was talking to that colored boy who works for your daddy."

It's starting to bother me the way Rayanne always refers to Gator as "that colored boy." She knows darn good and well what his name is. "That colored boy has a name," I say.

"Well for heaven's sake, I know that! It's Gator, right? That's not the point, Dove. We're talking about that girl, Rosemary."

When I don't say anything, Rayanne grabs my arm to stop me from taking another step until she can unload what's on her mind. She doesn't waste any words making her point this time. "We can't have trash sitting at our table at lunch. It makes us look bad."

We've reached the parking lot at Whelan's. I'm not about to get into a scene with Rayanne in front of all these people. The truth is, I can't pretend these exact same thoughts didn't go through my head earlier that day, because they did. More than once.

Whelan's is already packed with cars. Kids are sitting on the hoods or leaning against car doors, which usually means there's no place to sit inside. And there isn't. All the counter seats are taken and the booths are bulging with kids. Some are even sitting on each other's laps because there's not enough room. The seatless masses stand around clutching their glasses of Coke so they won't get them knocked out of their hands. "Stagger Lee" is playing on the jukebox, not that you can hear much of the song above all the noise.

From the outside Whelan's smells like hamburgers frying. Inside the only smell is cigarette smoke. It's so thick I can hardly see to the other end of the room.

I order two cherry Cokes and hand one to Rayanne. We head back out to the parking lot.

Rayanne spots Chase before I do. I think she has some sort of special homing device that zeros in on him just about anywhere. He's sitting in his T-bird with the top down, surrounded by a bunch of other seniors. Some are sitting on the hood, some in the backseat.

I lean against a two-toned black-and-white Chevy a few yards away and sip my cherry Coke, waiting for him to notice me. Rayanne parks herself on the hood.

Willy Podd's truck is two cars over from Chase's. He's got the door open and he's sitting sideways on the passenger side with his feet on the running board. Earl is leaning against the open door. I can't look at either of them without seeing their ugly faces looming over Rosemary at lunch earlier. I shift my attention to Chase. He's studying a road map he's got spread out on his steering wheel.

"Hey, Chase!" Willy shouts. "I think somebody's here to see you." He jerks his chin in my direction. I want to smack his creepy face.

Earl swaggers over and perches himself on the hood of Chase's car, bumping another kid out of his way. Willy follows him. He leans against the hood but doesn't get on it.

Chase doesn't pay either of them any mind. He's grinning over at me. He lifts a pack of cigarettes from the dashboard, sticks one cigarette behind his ear, flips open his Zippo and lights another one. "You here to hobnob with the hep crowd, Dove?" I ignore this. He knows I don't come to Whelan's after school.

I walk over to his car and stand by the passenger door. Rayanne slides from the hood of the Chevy and comes up beside me.

"Actually, I was hoping Earl here could give me lessons on how to be a hood ornament," I say.

Earl ignores this. But Chase laughs.

"Hear tell some nigger paid you a visit last night," Earl says. "Heard he set your barn on fire."

Willy is watching me with his squinty little eyes. He silently mouths the words *nigger lover.*

"Nobody set fire to our barn," I tell them. "It was lightning."

Willy starts rattling off at the mouth like some half-crazed jaybird. "Well, now . . . that's not how I heard it. Nope.

Uh-uh. I'm thinking more like somebody has it out for your daddy. One of the pickers, maybe." He looks over at Chase, like he's daring him to call him a liar. Chase keeps his eyes on that map of his. He's acting like Willy isn't even there.

I have this sudden need to feel something solid. I put my hand on Chase's side-view mirror. It's like putting my hand on a hot griddle, but I don't let go. "Since when did you start thinking?" I say.

Willy just laughs at that.

Earl laughs too. He pulls out his comb and runs it through his hair, which he's been trying to grow longer so it'll look like Willy's. He grins over at Rayanne.

Rayanne ignores him, as usual. She bends over, resting her arms on the passenger door, and says to Chase, "You see who it was?"

"It wasn't *anybody,* Rayanne," I say. I swear her brain goes on a vacation whenever she's around that boy. And it's starting to get on my nerves.

Chase doesn't bother to give Rayanne an answer. He folds up the map and sticks it in his glove compartment. Then he leans over and opens the door on the passenger side. "Come on," he says to me, "I'll give you a ride home."

"Tell them," I say to him, looking at all the kids who have gravitated over to Chase's car to find out what's going on. "Tell them it was lightning." I slam the car door shut and back away.

He takes a long drag from his cigarette. I notice he's taken the bandage off his hand. There's an angry red blister on the spot between his thumb and forefinger. "You all heard Dove, here. She says it was lightning."

Willy gives him a look, like he can't be sure whose side Chase is on. But then his lip curls up on one side in an ugly sneer. He's figured out Chase hasn't agreed with me, he's just repeated what I said.

Chase glances around a few times, then he tells everybody hanging around his car to get lost, that he and I have private business to discuss.

Earl slides off the hood. He and Willy head back to Willy's truck. They punch each other in the shoulder a few times and laugh.

Rayanne gives me a pleading look. I know she wants to stay. "Just give us a few minutes," I tell her. "Chase's got something he needs to explain." I hand her my empty glass.

As soon as Rayanne goes back inside Whelan's, I turn to Chase. "You know darn good and well it was lightning that set our barn on fire. Why didn't you just tell them outright?"

Chase leans over and flings open the passenger door again. "Come on, Dove. Get in."

"I'm staying right where I am till you tell me what's going on."

"I know that *you* said it was lightning. I never said one way or the other what caused that fire."

"If you saw somebody at our place last night, why didn't you tell me in the kitchen?" I stare down at the burn on his hand. "Did you tell my dad?"

"You want to hear what I got to say, then get in." He tosses the lighted cigarette across the parking lot, just missing one of the waitresses who is scurrying by. "I'll tell you on the way home."

There doesn't seem much point in being stubborn about

this. I get in the car. If nothing else, it saves me a two-mile walk.

It isn't until Chase is halfway out of the parking lot that I suddenly remember Rayanne. When I look back at the front window of Whelan's, there she is, looking for all the world like I've taken the last lifeboat and left her behind on a sinking ship.

"Wait. We forgot Rayanne."

"Dove, she lives right here in town. She knows her way home."

"But I can't just leave her there like that." I know I'm going to get an earful from her about this later.

Chase keeps on driving. With the top down, the wind blowing through my short hair tickles. It suddenly occurs to me that he hasn't once said anything about my hair. It's not like him to miss an opportunity to tease me.

"There isn't a single word of truth to what Willy said at Whelan's," I tell him.

"Course not." Chase leans back in his seat and rests his arm on the car door.

"Then why act like it's true?"

He flips on the radio and fiddles with the tuner till he finds the station he wants. "I like your hair," he says. "It looks good."

I search his face for hints of sarcasm and can't find a one. "Don't change the subject," I tell him. "You know what this town is like. Things are only going to get worse if you let them think it was a colored person who set fire to our barn. They'll get all riled up, making it out to be something it's not."

He drums his fingers on the steering wheel. "I didn't start this rumor, okay? I told you that this morning."

"If you didn't start this rumor, who did?" I already have a pretty good idea, based on what Rayanne told me in homeroom. I just want to hear it from Chase.

Chase shrugs and looks off to his left. His words float back to me, muffled by the wind. "Does it matter? The rumor's already out there. People will either believe it or they won't."

He is driving me crazy. "It was Willy Podd, wasn't it?"

Chase turns back to me. "Yeah, best I can tell."

I'm not surprised. Willy has never tried to hide his feelings about colored folks. He hates them and makes sure everybody knows it. There doesn't seem to be any rhyme or reason for him to hate coloreds. He just does. This latest story he's spreading around is just one more way of announcing his hate to the world. "You can't stand Willy Podd. Why are you letting him get away with telling lies about my barn?"

Chase reaches over and runs his hand along the back of my neck. His touch is gentle. I don't want him to stop. "Willy'd already started telling everybody his own version of what happened before I even got to school this morning."

"And you didn't say anything to stop him?"

"I tried, but by then everyone had pretty much bought into Willy's story. I told them it was lightning that caused the fire. But then Willy started in about how it sounded to him like I might be trying to cover for somebody. That got everybody all fired up about why I'd do something like that when things around here are getting—" Chase lets his hand drop from my neck and keeps his eyes on the road. The place where his hand has been feels suddenly cold.

"Getting what?" I ask.

"Look, Dove, this'll all blow over in a few days. Let it go, okay?"

"What's my dad going to think when he hears this?"

Chase shrugs. "He probably won't think anything at all. He knows what's been going on around here."

The strangest feeling comes over me when Chase says this. It doesn't sound as if he's talking about the usual stuff between coloreds and white folks. This is about something else. Something he and my dad know. And I don't.

Delia sets a piece of key lime pie in front of me on the kitchen table when I get home. She makes the best key lime pie in all of Florida.

She walks over to the screen door, folds her thick arms together, and makes little grunting noises at the piles of cinders that used to be our barn.

"Good thing your daddy had that new barn of his built a few years back."

A novel lies open on the table. I flip through the pages.

"Don't you go losing my place," Delia snaps.

I am just about to ask her if she's heard about those rumors Willy's been spreading when the phone rings.

"How could you leave me there like that!" Rayanne screams at me from the other end of the receiver.

"Rayanne," I say, "you live right there in town."

"You could have told me you were leaving."

"Chase pulled out before I had a chance. It wasn't on purpose." I'm eyeing my uneaten pie from across the room. I still have the fork in my hand. The phone cord won't stretch far enough for me to reach the pie. My mouth is watering. "I've got to go, Rayanne," I say.

"Whidden Hadley asked me to the senior prom," she says out of the blue.

The senior prom is a big deal, especially if you're only a sophomore and an upperclassman asks you to go. "When did he ask you?"

"This afternoon. At Whelan's."

"Well, now, see? That probably wouldn't have happened if you hadn't gone back inside to wait for me."

"Or he might have asked me some other time."

"Rayanne," I groan. "Aren't you excited?" Whidden Hadley has scummy teeth and breath so bad it could make a cow keel over. But he's got a sweet nature.

"Well of course I'm excited. Who wouldn't be? It's the senior prom."

This is followed by a long swell of silence. I'm thinking maybe she's hung up now that she's delivered her news.

"Rayanne?"

"Did Chase ask you to the prom?"

It takes me a minute to realize Rayanne thinks Chase drove off with me this afternoon so that he could ask me to the prom.

"No," I tell her. "And I don't expect he will." I don't bother to tell her that Chase isn't much for formal dances. Formal anything, for that matter.

Right about then somebody knocks on the screen door.

"Come on in, Gator," Delia shouts, not bothering to look to see if that's who's at the door. Gator usually shows up about this time every day, so it isn't any surprise.

He steps inside, carrying two big empty galvanized buckets. He lets the screen door bump against his shoulder, easing it closed. He nods my way, then crosses the kitchen and hands Delia the buckets, which she fills with water for the picking crew.

"Hey, Gator," I say.

Gator's staring out the kitchen window as if there is something going on outside he doesn't want to miss. He looks over his shoulder at me and nods again. The gash in his forehead is less puckered today.

"Gator?" Rayanne says. "You mean that colored boy?"

"I have to go, Rayanne." I hang up before she can say another word.

Delia opens the cabinet under the sink and pulls out a stack of paper sacks. Gator gets this smile on his face like she's about to hand him one of her key lime pies. I suddenly realize I've missed that old grin of his. I don't recall him smiling all that much lately.

Gator tucks the bags under one arm as Delia hands him the filled buckets. He takes everything out to the porch and comes back with two more empty pails.

"Here, Gator," I say, grabbing the plate of pie from the table and giving it to him. "Have some pie." I have no idea what made me do that. I guess I was hoping to see Gator's face light up again. But he only looks confused.

Delia eyes me suspiciously. She thinks I'm up to something, which I'm not.

Gator stands there holding the pie like he's afraid it might explode if he makes one false move. I pass him the fork I'm still holding. "It's clean," I tell him. "I didn't use it yet."

He gets this amused look on his face.

Delia sets the last of the buckets by Gator's feet. "You go on out on the porch and eat that," she tells him.

Gator doesn't say a word. He just heads outside and dives right into that pie. I watch him through the screen door.

"What you up to?" Delia asks.

"Nothing."

"Doesn't look like nothing from where I'm standing."

"I thought he'd like some pie is all." I go over to the counter where the rest of the pie sits and cut myself another slice.

Gator's back in less than a minute, empty plate in hand. He takes the other two buckets out to the porch. I stand at the back door and watch him carry them to the trailer that's attached to one of our tractors. Eli's sitting on the tractor, waiting for him. He lifts his cap and slides his arm across his forehead. When he gets down to help Gator with the buckets, I notice his movements are slow and stiff.

"Delia," I say, "you heard any rumors about our barn?"

She tears off a piece of aluminum foil to cover what's left of the pie and stands there holding it. "What kind of rumors?"

"About how it might not have been lightning that caused the fire?" I savor the sweet tartness of the pie on my tongue, rolling it around in my mouth.

The foil in her hand makes metallic rustling noises. "What you talkin' about? Are folks saying it was something else?"

"Good Lord Almighty! Stop answering my questions with questions."

Delia slaps the aluminum foil over the top of the pie and tucks it in. Then she grabs a wet dishrag and begins wiping the counter. She's working at it so hard I'm sure she's going to wear a hole in the Formica. "Don't you have some homework to do?"

Another question. I sigh and go back to enjoying my pie.

* * * * * * * * * * * * * * * * *

By the end of the week, things seem to have settled down again. The kids at school have stopped asking me to tell them the story about my barn. Rosemary Howell has stopped stalking me in the halls between classes, and there haven't been any more fires.

As soon as the last bell rings, I head for the cemetery to read to Tory Ray Allister. It's his turn. I try to be fair and give everyone equal time.

Tory's headstone is set way back behind the church, a few feet from the stone wall. It's quiet and shady here. I lean against the side of the tombstone and begin reading from this book of medieval English verse I found in the library.

> Love is soft and love is sweet, and speaks in accents
>   fair;
> Love is mighty agony, and love is mighty care;
> Love is utmost ecstasy and love is keen to dare;
> Love is wretched misery; to live with, it's despair.

"Maybe you aren't missing much after all, Tory," I tell him.

From nowhere this voice says, "And just how would you know that?"

The voice rockets me to my feet. I'm shaking from the roots of my hair to my toenails. Then I hear someone laughing and turn around to find Gator sitting on the stone wall. He swings his bare feet, bumping his heels against the rocks. His knees poke through the holes in his dungarees. He's got on his red T-shirt and suddenly I'm reminded of the storm last week.

"What are you doing here?" I ask.

Gator shrugs. "Listening to you read poems and talk to dead folks." He gets this snide little grin on his face.

"I am *not* talking to dead folks. I'm thinking out loud is all."

"Sure you are."

I pick up my book, brush the dirt and grass away, and slap it shut. "That *was* you last week, wasn't it? Here in the cemetery."

"You should've seen your face," Gator says. He laughs, thinking about this.

I am not amused. "Are you spying on me or something?"

"What's there to spy on? Some white girl reading bad— *real* bad—poems to a dead person who can't even get up and walk away if he wants to?" He reaches in his back pocket and pulls out a rolled-up piece of brown paper sack. He smooths it open. It's a drawing of the church with part of the cemetery and stone wall—a real good drawing. He's got the perspective just right.

"Not bad," I tell him.

"Better than that dumb poem you were reading."

I ignore this. "So that's why you've been coming here? To draw?"

Gator doesn't answer me. He takes his good sweet time rolling up his picture. "You know that poem you read last week—the one about fears and dying?"

"'When I have fears that I may cease to be'?"

"Yeah, that one. It wasn't half bad. Not good, just not as bad as the one you read today."

I don't know when it happened, but somewhere between looking at Gator's drawing and talking about poetry, I must have hopped up on the wall. Right now I am sitting only inches away from him.

He lifts the book of medieval English verse from my hands, flips through it, and shakes his head. "You can keep this one," he says.

Something has been on my mind ever since he confirmed it really was him in the cemetery the week before. "How'd you get back to the groves so fast last week?" I ask.

"Ran like the devil was on my heels," Gator says. "That's how."

It was possible, I guess. I did take my time getting into Chase's car. Then I wandered around the groves for a while before I actually saw Gator.

He is studying me with this strange look on his face.

"You thought I came out to the groves to tell Travis on you, didn't you?"

"You didn't?"

"No!"

"Just out for a stroll, then?"

"I happen to like walking in the groves. Not that it's any of your business."

We eye each other. Neither of us looks away. We're sizing up the situation. We both know we shouldn't be here, talking to each other. But we're doing it all the same.

I slide from the wall.

Gator jumps down too. "That the only book you got?"

I sit down on the grass next to Tory Ray's headstone. There's a huge hole and a run in my stocking, probably from sitting on the stone wall. I tuck my legs under my skirt. "It's the only book of poems I've got with me."

"What else you got?" he says.

I show him my geometry book. He nods, but I can see he's not interested.

"What's that?" he says, pointing to another book sitting on top of my loose-leaf binder.

"My history book."

He reaches over and picks it up. He runs his finger up and down the contents pages, then flips to the index. His finger continues its search. When he doesn't find whatever it is he's looking for, he hands it back. "You're right, it is *your* history book."

I can't be sure what he means by that. "You want to hear some epitaphs?" I ask.

"Some what?"

"Epitaphs. They're these poems and sentiments you find on people's gravestones."

Gator stares at me for a few seconds, as if he can't be sure whether or not I'm pulling his leg. I open my notebook and show him some of the epitaphs I collected for Miss Poyer's class. He reads the one about Rowena Mae Cunningham and laughs.

"Okay, let's hear 'em." He leans his back against the stone wall, making himself at home, while I read him epitaphs. It's kind of nice, having a live person to read poems to for a change.

There is something comfortable and familiar about being here with Gator. It's not the same as when we were kids, playing in the groves. But still, sitting here on the grass, laughing ourselves sick over some of the epitaphs I read to him, reminds me of those other times and how much fun we used to have before my dad and Jacob Tully and a few other folks decided to put a stop to it. Back when Gator was this boy I liked to play with. Back before I began thinking of him as one of the pickers—just somebody who worked for my dad.

I flip through my notebook and find one of my favorites, an epitaph for Matthew Peas, who died in 1874.

PEAS NOT HERE
JUST THE POD
PEAS SHELLED OUT
AND WENT TO GOD

From behind us comes the sound of giggling. Gator and I aren't the only ones laughing. When I turn to look, there is Rosemary Howell, leaning against a tree.

My first thought is that she's still following me around. And I'm not sure how to put a stop to that. Gator, though, doesn't seem at all surprised that she's here. Or worried—

which we both should be, considering what happened last Saturday across from the movie theater. He just smiles at her and nods. Rosemary smiles back and then comes to sit with us.

"Well," I tell them, closing up my books and brushing myself off. "It's almost dinnertime. Delia's going to wonder where I've got to." I am expecting Rosemary to get up too. Maybe walk part of the way with me since I'll be going past Luellen's shop. But she doesn't move a muscle, except to give me a little wave goodbye.

12

On Sunday after church Rayanne, Jinny, and I decide to head over to Whelan's for a soda. The place has an entirely different atmosphere on Sundays. Usually it's packed with families that stop in after church for a late breakfast. It's nothing like it is on weekdays after school.

Rayanne walks along, talking a blue streak about Whidden Hadley and the prom. I tune her out. Jinny takes care of all the polite responses. But then Rayanne starts in on the migrant workers and how they've been stirring up trouble. That gets my attention.

"What kind of trouble?" I ask.

"Well, for heaven's sake, Dove, don't you know

what's been going on in your own backyard? Where you been?"

I'm not sure how to answer this. "What *kind* of trouble?" I ask again.

"Well, they've been boycotting the camp store, for one thing." She flings her gloved hand up in the air, dismissing the whole thing. "They're only hurting themselves."

"From what I hear, the camp store charges three times what the Winn-Dixie does for the same groceries," Jinny says.

I look over at her. Sometimes Jinny surprises me.

"Well, then, no wonder they're shopping someplace else," I say. "If they can save money, why not?"

"And that's another thing." Rayanne adjusts the blue net on her hat, pulling it farther down over her eyes. "The money. They're complaining about not getting paid on time and having some of their wages withheld because they owe money to the store. Well, if they owe money, they got to pay up like everybody else. Isn't that right, Jinny?"

Jinny is walking on my other side. She slips off her white gloves—setting her charm bracelet to jingling—and stuffs them in her purse, all the while looking thoughtful. But she doesn't say anything.

"Well, if they're not getting paid on time, that's not right," I say. I can't believe I haven't heard about this sooner. Although, thinking back, Gator did say something about the store when we were talking in the groves last week. What he didn't bother to tell me was that there's been trouble.

"I wouldn't be the least bit surprised if it's the pickers who've been setting those fires, like everybody says. Just to get back at Travis Waite and them," Rayanne prattles on. "My daddy says if somebody doesn't put a lid on it soon, this whole thing could boil over and make a real mess."

Rayanne's dad is president of the Benevolence Savings and Loan. He's in a good position to know just about everybody's business around here, including the folks who own the camp store.

"A lid on what?" I ask. "Rayanne, you're not making any sense."

She doesn't answer. We've turned onto Main Street and a familiar silver-blue T-bird is coming our way. Rayanne grabs my arm.

"Ooo, it's Chase. Do something. Wave!"

"You've got arms. Wave to him yourself," I tell her.

Right about then Chase pulls his T-bird up to the curb next to us.

"Hey, Rayanne. Jinny." He shifts his eyes my way and grins. "Hey, Dove."

My heart does a happy little skip. Lately it's been doing that whenever Chase shows up unexpectedly.

Rayanne leans against the passenger side door. "We've been talking about the pickers," she says.

"Yeah?" Chase looks straight ahead through his windshield. I can tell he's not all that interested in what Rayanne has to say. It dawns on me that he probably already knows what's going on.

"I could use a ride home," I tell him. "If you're heading in that direction."

Rayanne snaps to attention and shoots me a look. "I thought we were going to Whelan's." She glares at me, then looks over at Chase. "You want to come with us?" she asks.

"Dove here needs a ride home," he says.

Rayanne's fury—hotter than the heat rising from the sidewalk—radiates all around me as I slip into the front seat of Chase's car. "Say hey to Whidden for me," I call back to her as we pull off.

I settle myself into the soft bucket seat. I know the T-bird is going to fly like the wind the second we are outside the town limits, so I take off my hat, which is nothing more than a little wedge of pink with tiny white flowers and a pink veil that matches my pink sheath dress.

"Do you know anything about what's going on with the pickers and the camp store?" I ask Chase before we are halfway down the block.

He looks over at me. "Where'd you hear that?"

"Rayanne."

"Right. Rayanne Beecham. The Louella Parsons of Panther County. What'd she say?"

I tell him.

"I don't know much more than that myself," he says.

"I have a feeling there's more to this than a few upset pickers arguing about their wages going to pay their store bill."

Chase shrugs. "Maybe." He reaches over and rests his hand on mine. My heart is pounding double-time. "You want to see something that'll make your eyes pop out?" he asks.

"I have to get home. Delia's waiting on dinner." Delia always cooks us a big Sunday dinner, then she has the rest of the afternoon off. If I'm late, I'll never hear the end of it.

"Come on, Dove. It'll be fun."

"What is it?" I have to admit, I'm curious.

"I can't tell you. I have to show you."

"Delia'll have a fit if this cuts into her afternoon off."

"It's not gonna take all that long."

"Well, I guess it's okay," I tell him.

He switches on the radio and "All I Have to Do Is Dream" comes on. There doesn't seem to be much else to do but sit back, listen to the Everly Brothers, and wait to see where Chase is taking me.

After a while, I say, "Who runs that camp store, anyway?"

"Are you on that again?"

"So what if I am? I want to know is all."

Chase starts slapping one palm against the steering wheel, keeping time to a Jerry Lee Lewis song that has come on. "Travis Waite owns the store. He owns the whole camp."

"Travis Waite? He's their crew boss!"

"Oh, come on. Don't tell me you didn't know that."

"Why would I? Travis Waite works for my dad, not me. It's not like he's somebody I give any thought to, much less care what he does."

Chase shrugs. "So what's the big deal, then? A lot of crew leaders run camps."

"Well, how can they be crew bosses and also run the camps and stores?"

"They've got folks working for them. Like Travis. He's got Moss's brother, Tyler, and Jimmy's girlfriend, Maybeth Spencer, taking care of the store."

"So he offers the pickers credit. The pickers buy the things they need, and then the cost is taken out of their pay. Is that how it works?"

"Pretty much."

"Maybe they're getting cheated. Maybe that's what they're upset about."

"What is this? Are you writing a book?"

This is Chase's way of letting me know he's finished answering my questions, so I let it drop.

A short time later we turn off the main highway and head down a badly paved road. We bump over crater-sized potholes, pass by groves and open meadows. When we come to the bottom of a hill, Chase stops the car. "Watch this," he says.

I'm sure Chase has lost his mind, stopping the car in the middle of the road where just about anybody can come barreling down the hill and smash right into us. But he doesn't seem all that worried.

I give him a funny look.

"Just wait," he says.

I stare down at my white high heels, flex the pointed toes, and do as he says. I wait. All of a sudden the car begins to roll backward. *Uphill!*

My mouth must have dropped open all the way to my knees. Chase has been watching me, I guess waiting to see what I'd do. Now he throws his head back and bellows out a laugh.

"Spook Hill!" I shout. "This is Spook Hill, right?" I've heard about this place all my life, but I've never actually been here. Now I'm seeing it with my own eyes, feeling it with my own body. And it really exists. Stopped cars actually do roll backward up the hill. I've heard that some folks have even set balls at the bottom of the road just to watch them roll uphill. It's impossible, but it's true. It's like the laws of physics somehow skipped this spot. It's also downright spooky, which is more than likely how the place got its name.

"How does it work?" I ask.

Chase shakes his head. "Nobody knows." He's still grinning. He's so darn happy about surprising me that he can hardly contain himself.

"But there's got to be an explanation."

"Why? Why not just let it be a mystery? Something to wonder about." He leans toward me, gently trailing his fingers along the back of my neck. "Like why we care about the people we do," he whispers close to my ear.

My whole body goes soft. I know I should make him start up the car right this minute. I know Delia is going to have a fit. But I don't seem to have the will to move.

Chase's lips, gently pressing mine, are as much a surprise as Spook Hill. Soft and easy, sending warm waves rolling under my skin. After that first kiss, my mind must have shut down because the only thing I remember from that afternoon—besides Delia chewing me up one side and down the other for being late—is Chase Tully's touch.

13

On Monday Chase shows up at my locker after my first class to see if I want to go to the drive-in that night. *Some Like It Hot* is playing. I am pretty sure Chase picked this movie on account of Marilyn Monroe being in it. But I don't mind.

With him standing there smiling, leaning against the locker next to mine, I almost forget my dad's rule about not going out on school nights. And the drive-in is definitely out, no matter what night of the week it is.

I am having a hard time getting it through my head that Chase is asking me on a date. A *real* date. It's all I can do to think straight. "My dad won't let me go out on a school night," I tell him.

Chase just shrugs and says, "No big deal." Then he heads down the hall.

I want to go after him, grab him by the arm and say, "Hey, you ever hear of weekends?" But I don't.

For the rest of the day all I can think about is how I messed up my chance to go out with Chase. And how he will probably never ask me out again. If I'd been thinking clearly, I might have told him I'd try to figure a way to sneak out of the house and meet him someplace.

Fortunately Chase must have been thinking along those same lines because long about nine o'clock that night, I hear gravel raining down on the upper part of my bedroom window. I am still up, studying for a history test. When I look out the window, there is Chase, grinning up at me.

He points to the oak tree next to my window. I know he wants me to sneak down, but I'm not much for climbing trees these days.

I do a quick check in the mirror, turn out my light so Dad will think I'm asleep, close the door, and tiptoe downstairs. Dad is asleep on the couch in the living room, snoring. The TV is still on.

I slip out the back door. Chase is waiting for me. "I've got the car parked down at the end of the road," he says.

"I wasn't planning on going anywhere," I tell him. I'm wearing shorts and sneakers. Not exactly appropriate dating attire for young ladies. Delia would just up and die if she knew. "And if anybody sees us, Dad'll find out for sure."

Chase shakes his head. "He won't find out. I've got it all arranged."

Well, now, you have to be curious about something like

that, so I follow him down to the T-bird. Chase heads straight for town and parks behind the movie theater on Main Street. The marquee lights are dimmed. The place is closed. They only have a seven-o'clock show on weekdays.

I'm about to ask him what he thinks he's doing, when he says, "Just wait, okay?" He takes my hand and leads me to the back door. As soon as he pulls out a key, I know what's going on. His cousin, Billy Tyler, who is in my grade at school, has been working the Saturday matinees since he was thirteen. Billy's father—Chase's uncle—Will Tyler, owns the theater.

"You got that from Billy," I say. Chase grins at me and steps aside to let me in the door.

We hear swooshing sounds coming from inside the theater. Buford Radcliff is sweeping candy wrappers and stale popcorn from between the rows. Buford is as old as Methuselah. Half the time he forgets to put his teeth in, like tonight. Only a few wispy strands of white hair float around the top of his practically bald head as he moves back and forth. He looks like a skeleton in baggy clothes.

Chase puts a finger up to his lips. He points toward the projection room. We both hunker down and sneak up the side aisle by the wall. Buford is humming show tunes from *Oklahoma!* while he sweeps. He never even looks our way. We make it up to the dark room and watch from the window until he's finished for the night. Chase stands by the open door, listening until we hear the click of Buford's key and the slap of the back door.

Then Chase takes a reel of film and sets up the projector.

"What are you doing?" I ask.

"What does it look like I'm doing? We're going to watch a movie."

"You sure you know how to work that thing?"

"I've helped Uncle Will do this hundreds of times."

I have my doubts about it being that many times, but when beams of light carry those images down to the screen below, and suddenly there's John Wayne in *Rio Bravo*, well, I have to believe Chase knows what he's doing. We watch the entire movie from upstairs in the projection room. It would be a lot more romantic if we were sitting in the seats down below, instead of on these hard stools, where Chase could put his arm around me or hold my hand or maybe kiss me like he did at Spook Hill the day before, but he just sits by the projector on that dumb stool, watching John Wayne and Ricky Nelson. It's as if he's forgotten he brought me along.

When the movie is over and he's put the film back in the can, I say, "It's late. My dad's probably in bed by now. I have to get home."

Chase nods and we slip back downstairs into the theater. Except this time when he takes my hand, he steers me away from the back door and over to this archway beside the stage. He pulls the curtain aside, revealing a hallway behind it. The wall is stone, same as the foundation of the theater, and there are dim lights overhead. It's a little like walking through a tunnel.

Downstairs, beneath the stage, are all these old dressing rooms. Chase tells me they are from back when they used to have vaudeville acts before the movie came on. I have been coming to this movie theater since I was five years old and Dad took me to see *Snow White and the Seven Dwarfs*. All these years I never knew about these secret rooms tucked away below the stage.

Chase pulls down one of the musty old mattresses with gray-and-white ticking that are piled against one wall, and we spend the next hour making out. With Chase, kissing is everything I always imagined it would be. Even better.

The next night Chase shows up beneath my window again.

"I have to finish this paper on Thomas Jefferson for history tomorrow," I tell him.

Two minutes later I'm climbing down the oak outside my window, against my better judgment of course, and we drive into town again. But instead of going to the movie theater, Chase parks the T-bird at the railroad station. Across the way is a park. It's only a small park, with a big old mulberry tree in the middle. Folks around here say this is where all the public hangings used to take place before things got "civilized" and they started executing criminals at the state prison.

The mulberry tree is not exactly the most romantic spot in town, but it has its advantages. For instance, not too many people come here at night. They say the spirits of the dead—the ones who swung from the mulberry tree branches at the end of a rope—are still lurking about waiting to murder their next victim. So as you can imagine, the park is a pretty private place after dark.

For the next week and a half, Chase and I either sneak into the movie theater and head straight for the old dressing rooms, or we sit on a partially hidden bench near the mulberry tree. I don't care about homework or my grades or anything else. There is only one thing on my mind these days: Chase Tully.

. . . .

Rosemary Howell is hovering by the front door, waiting for me one afternoon as I'm leaving school.

"Can I talk to you a minute?" she says.

Her expression is so darned earnest, it makes me nervous. "Well . . . sure."

She falls into step beside me as I make my way across the lawn toward the school buses.

"Something happened last week. It has to do with one of your pickers. I thought maybe—"

"One of our pickers?"

Rosemary nods. Her shoulders are hunched over from the weight of all the books she's carrying. She shifts them around, balancing them on her hip. The books have left deep red gouges on her arms.

"Who?" I'm wondering if maybe she's talking about old Eli, or maybe Gator, and I start to worry.

Rosemary looks over at the kids running past us, heading for the buses. "Not here, okay? You want to come over to Luellen's with me?"

I watch the school buses. One by one the bus drivers rev up their engines. By the time the last bus leaves, I am on my way down Main Street heading to Luellen's with Rosemary.

Luellen's apartment is above her shop. Rosemary and I go through a door wedged between the beauty shop and Tuckett's Hardware. When we reach the upper landing, I get a strong whiff of rutabaga. It about makes me gag.

Rosemary sets her books on the landing, fumbles around in her purse, and pulls out a key. The odor of rutabaga wallops me in the face the second Rosemary unlocks the door. The door opens right into Luellen's living room. To my left is the kitchen. Something is simmering on the burner. My guess would be rutabaga.

Rosemary dumps her books on the kitchen table and

heads for the stove. She lifts the lid, then picks up the wooden spoon lying on the counter and stirs the contents. "Salt pork and rutabaga," she says, as if I haven't already figured that out. As if everybody in the beauty shop downstairs *and* in Tuckett's Hardware *and* probably half of Main Street haven't already figured that out. "Luellen must have just put it on."

There isn't any reasonable response to this, so I just stand there and wait.

"Make yourself to home," Rosemary says. She seems a little fidgety. I can tell she's not used to having company. She doesn't seem to have any friends at school. Every time I see her, she's alone. Maybe she has spent so much time picking fruit with her family and moving from place to place, and working at other jobs, like washing people's hair at Luellen's, that she doesn't know how to act around the kids at school.

The sofa bed is still open, exposing a tangle of sheets. I look over at the only other chair. It is buried under a mountain of wrinkled clothes. I sit on the coffee table instead, shoving aside a mess of fashion magazines to make room.

Luellen's apartment reminds me of a trailer home, only wider. At first it looks to be just the living room connected to the kitchen. But now I can see a short hallway to the left, off the kitchen, which probably leads to the bathroom and Luellen's bedroom.

Rosemary turns on the radio and takes two bottles of RC Cola from the fridge. She opens them, hands me one, and stares down at my coffee table seat. "We can sit in the kitchen, if you want," she offers.

My backside is already getting numb. "Good plan," I say. I sit across from her at the kitchen table. "Lonesome

Town" is playing on the radio. Ricky Nelson's voice echoes off the walls of Luellen's apartment.

"Don't you just love this song?" Rosemary asks.

"Rosemary, you wanted to tell me about one of our pickers, remember?"

She stares down at her soda. "Something happened over at the camp," she says, finally. "Somebody, some . . . men set fire to a clothesline full of clothes. They came through in trucks, blasting their horns. One of them hung out the window with a lighted torch. He set all these clothes on fire."

My fingers are clenched around the RC bottle. The icy chill seeps into them; it races through my whole body. "Is everybody okay? I mean, nobody got hurt, did they?"

"I don't think so. It was more like a warning. Some of the other pickers formed a bucket brigade, hauling water from the taps. There wasn't anything left, nothing but some soggy, charred pieces of cloth, lying in little piles on the ground."

"Why are you telling me this?" I ask.

"Well, because those clothes? They belonged to Julio Gonzalez and his family. Someone said Julio and his wife work in your daddy's groves."

I remember overhearing those two men speaking in Spanish in our groves a while back. Gator had called the barrel-shaped man Julio. I'm pretty sure he said Julio Gonzalez.

"How come you know all this? Is your family staying at the same migrant camp or something?"

Rosemary shakes her head. If she's suprised that I know her folks are pickers, she doesn't let on. "White pickers don't usually live in those camps," she says. "They generally keep to themselves. Camp out somewheres, like my folks do. They don't like to be beholden to the crew leaders any more than they have to be. Some live in the white section of the camps, if there is one. Mostly there isn't.

"My family lives in a trailer. Sometimes the owners of the groves they're working in let them camp on their land. Depends. Some are real nice about it. Others don't want any of the pickers living that close by."

"Then you didn't actually see these men set fire to the clothes?"

"No."

"Well, if you weren't there, how did you find out about this? How do you even know if it's true?"

Rosemary takes a deep breath, as if she's about to go off the high dive. "A friend told me. Somebody I trust."

What I'm trying to figure out is why Rosemary is coming to me with this story about the Gonzalez family. It's not as if I know these people.

"Why didn't you just go to the police? Why tell me?"

Rosemary slumps in her chair. She rolls her bottle of RC back and forth between her palms. Maybe she is thinking she's made a mistake. That I'm not the person she should have told her story to.

"This friend, he thought you should know." She takes a long swallow of soda. "He thought you might be interested in what's happening to some of your pickers is all. Maybe even thought you could help."

"This friend wouldn't happen to be Gator, would it?"

She looks away. And I know I'm right.

"That day, in the cemetery, you didn't just happen to be walking by, did you?"

Rosemary glances up at the clock above the sink. She is on her feet in a flash. "Omigosh! I'm late for work." She heads for the living room and starts digging through the mess of clothes on the chair. She pulls out her blue uniform and white apron. I stare hard at that apron. "How long have you and Gator been . . . friends?" Even I can hear the disapproval in my voice. But I can't help what I'm feeling right now. Rosemary and Gator, seeing each other, well, it's just plain unnatural.

Rosemary holds up the wrinkled uniform. "Luellen's gonna kill me when she sees this. I don't have time to iron it." She slips out of her school dress and pulls the uniform over her head.

"Rosemary! I'm talking to you."

"Sorry. I've gotta go." And she is out the door before I can say another word.

Walking home from Luellen's place, it suddenly dawns on me that setting fire to the migrants' clothes and trying to scare them sounds like something the Klan would do. I remember this photograph Billy Tyler passed around school every chance he had, back when we were in the fifth grade. He said he got it from his cousin in Alabama when he was spending the summer with his aunt and uncle. The photograph showed this colored man hanging from a tree limb. Off to the far right of the picture you could just make out part of a white robe and hood. Billy was real proud of that picture.

Up until then I never knew much if anything about the Ku Klux Klan. When I asked my dad, all he said was, there are some angry people who use organizations like that to hurt others. He told me the Klan had disbanded after World War Two and wasn't around anymore. But that didn't help much. I still had nightmares for weeks after that.

I push these thoughts out of my head real quick. The Klan would never be in a place like Benevolence, Florida.

Delia is vacuuming the living room when I get home. She has a book in one hand, the handle of the vacuum cleaner in the other, and she is humming some tune I don't recognize. I stand in the archway in the foyer, watching her and thinking about what Rosemary told me.

Seems to me, the more I think about it, that maybe Willy Podd and his friends might be behind what happened over at the migrant camp. I wouldn't put something like that past them.

I sit down on the couch. Even with her eyes on the book, Delia maneuvers the vacuum cleaner without hitting a single piece of furniture.

When Delia finally turns the vacuum cleaner in my direction and sees me sitting there, her gasp about empties the room of every ounce of air.

She flips the switch off and rests both hands on her hips. "You trying to send me to an early grave?"

When I don't answer, she says, "You got something on your mind?"

"No."

"Well, then, I got work to do." The vacuum cleaner roars into action.

"Yes!" I shout. "I do have something on my mind."

She flicks the switch off again and stands with one hand on her hip, staring me down.

I wasn't planning on asking her about Gus. I wasn't even thinking about him. But for some reason his face popped into my head the exact minute Delia asked me if I had something on my mind. Only now that I have her attention, I don't know how to begin.

"Well, come on then, tell me what it is if you're gonna. I haven't got all day."

"I want to hear about Gus," I tell her. "About how he died?"

Delia's back goes rigid. She bends down to unplug the vacuum cleaner cord. "You on that again?"

I know she will try to run me off like she usually does. Only I don't plan on giving in this time.

Delia leaves the vacuum cleaner where it is, sets her book on the dining room table, and heads for the kitchen.

I follow right behind her. "Please, Delia. I want to know."

She rests her hands on the edge of the sink. For the

longest time she stares out the window at the groves beyond. Then she lifts a colander of green beans from the sink, fills a pot with water, and sits down at the table.

I sit across from her and wait.

"You remember how Gus loved playing that beat-up old sax of his?" She snaps a bean into four small pieces and drops them in the pot.

"Course I do." Sometimes, while Gus was waiting to take Delia home, he would sit on the steps of our back porch playing his saxophone, making these mournful sounds that came right up out of his belly into his mouth and through that sax for the whole world to hear.

"Well, our boy, Jeremiah, he'd been accepted to this college. A real good school."

"What school was that?"

"Howard University up there in Washington, D.C."

"I've heard of it." All I really know is that it's a college for colored folks.

"Jeremiah was working summers digging ditches to save money for school. It paid better than picking oranges. We knew we didn't have enough money to send him for the whole four years. So Gus, he took on extra jobs. Did some picking for your daddy till the season ended. Then on weekends he played with this jazz band over at Cholly Blue's juke joint. Cholly always had live music on weekends. Mostly they turned into jamming sessions, but they were good."

I know the place Delia is talking about. White folks don't go to Cholly's. It's over in the colored section of town, on the west side. But I know some kids from school who sometimes hang out in the woods behind Cholly's just to listen to the music.

Delia goes right on snapping beans. She keeps her eyes glued on them. You would think those beans were the most important thing in the world to her right now.

Then she starts talking again. "Gus was walking home about two in the morning from Cholly's, on account of our car was in the shop. He had his saxophone case in his hand, with that sweater I told you about tied around it. He was walking along the side of the road, coming up to our street. He was getting ready to cross to the other side when this car came tearing like streaked lightning round the corner, weaving all over the place. And it was heading straight for Gus.

"Well, about that time Cholly was coming up the road in his car, right behind these drunken fools, and he swears they were aiming their car, like some big old cannon, straight for my poor Gus. One of them was leaning out the window, whooping and hollering and slapping his hand on the door. Cholly said Gus tried to jump out of the way, but the car swerved and hit him anyway."

Delia looks over at me. The lids of her eyes are half closed. It feels as if somebody has grabbed hold of my heart and is squeezing the daylights out of it. I can hardly breathe. Delia stops snapping beans. She rests her wrists on the edge of the colander, letting her hands dangle there.

"By the time Cholly got to him, Gus was almost dead. But we didn't know that then. He was unconscious and busted up real bad. Part of the side of his face was tore off. Cholly came running up to the house, half outta his mind, pounding on the door till he got me out of bed.

"I was in my old bathrobe. I remember thinking I had to put on shoes, but I couldn't think where they were. An old pair of Gus's work boots was in the hall, there. So I slipped my feet into them, and me and Cholly—Jeremiah had the car, he was off with his friends somewheres—we got Gus into the backseat of Cholly's car.

"I held Gus's head in my lap. The tore-up side was facing down, so he just looked like his old self to me. I kept talking to him, telling him to hold on, everything was going to be all right. I didn't know Gus was already dead by then."

Delia tilts her head back, rolling her eyes toward the ceiling. "Well, now, looking back on it, maybe I did know. I guess I just didn't want to believe it. All I could think was that we were taking him to the hospital so the doctors could patch him up.

"But those doctors in the emergency room, all they did was tell me Gus was dead. I guess there wasn't much else for them to do.

"All I remember after that is looking down at my bathrobe and seeing Gus's blood all over it, soaked right through to my nightgown, which was sticking to my skin where the blood had started drying.

"Next day Cholly tried to tell the police about how Gus's dying was a hit-and-run, seeing as how whoever it was in that car kept right on going, like Gus wasn't anything more than a bump in the road. Never even stopped to look back. But nobody paid Cholly any mind. Especially since he didn't get the license plate number of the car."

I slump down in my chair. "It sounds like the person driving the car was drunk."

"Probably was, but aiming that car straight at my Gus, stepping on the gas like he did . . . that man knew what he was doing.

"Cholly, he thought he recognized one of the men who was in that car, the one hanging out the window. It was a white man, for sure. He didn't have any doubt about that at all. But he didn't see who the driver was, and he couldn't remember what kind of car it was either. Didn't belong to anybody he knew. All he could remember was that it was a dark-colored sedan. Cholly knew those men hadn't come to our section of town for any other reason than to cause trouble.

"The police said they'd check Cholly's story with the man he thought he recognized. But the man said he wasn't anywhere near that part of town that night. Said he wouldn't have been caught dead in the colored quarters. Only he didn't call it 'colored.' Seems he had an alibi. Must have, cause nothing happened after that."

Delia is done telling her story. She doesn't look at me now; she is ripping into those beans like she's tearing the limbs off a plucked chicken.

I come over to her side of the table, put my arms around her shoulders, and bend down so I can press my forehead against the back of her neck like I used to do when I was little.

I'm not sure I can trust myself to talk. A heavy sadness seeps into me. Sadness for Gus and for Delia and for Jeremiah. For all Gus and Delia's children. "So they never caught the person who killed Gus?" I whisper this into her neck.

Delia gives one sharp sideways swing of her head, as if to

put an end to this whole discussion. I unwind my arms from her shoulders and back away.

"But Cholly thought he recognized one of them," I remind her.

Delia gets up and slams the pot of broken beans on the stove. "Now, do you really think that matters to white folks? Especially when it was white folks that Cholly was pointing his finger at?"

Delia looks me right in the eye. She is daring me to take their side, the white folks who killed her Gus.

"I'm sorry about what happened to Gus, Delia. I truly am. Who was it Cholly saw?"

Delia shrugs. "He never did tell me, seeing as how it turned out the man had an alibi. Cholly just figured he'd made a mistake."

"Those men, whoever they are, should be in jail."

"Sweet baby Jesus. Haven't you figured out yet there's two kinds of justice in this world? There's justice for the white folks and a whole other justice for coloreds."

"Delia," I plead, "find out who it was Cholly thought he recognized, and I'll get my dad—"

Delia chokes out a laugh. At least I think it's a laugh. It's hard to tell. "Lord, child, sometimes I just don't know what to make of you." For some reason I have this feeling Delia isn't talking about just me but about every white person she has ever known.

She waves her hand at me. "Go on, now. You better get to your homework."

As I turn to leave I remember what she said the last time I brought up Gus, about having her reasons for wearing his clothes, about how it makes her feel close to him, like he is still with her. "Remember when you said you had your reasons for wearing Gus's clothes?"

Delia nods at me suspiciously.

"You only gave me one reason. You got others?"

"That's none of your business. I told you enough already. More'n you needed to hear. Now go on, git."

I give in and head upstairs. For the longest while I stand by my bedroom window, looking out over the groves. Close to seven hundred acres of orange trees lined up in tidy rows like soldiers on the march. In the distance I see some of the pickers in the back of Travis's produce truck. They are packed in like cattle. They stand, some with their arms stuck through the openings, holding on to the wood slats to keep from losing their balance. Travis is taking his crew back to the camp. When he's not hauling them around in that produce truck, he drives this old blue Ford pickup with a skunk tail flying from the radio antenna.

The late-afternoon sun is pouring through my bedroom window, making this soft cloud of drifting motes of dust in the light. I watch the truck as it comes near the house. Gator is pressed up against the ropes across the back of the truck. Even from here I can tell it's him. I recognize the faded red T-shirt.

That's when it comes to me.

Maybe this is why Delia wears Gus's clothes, one of those reasons she doesn't want to tell me about. Maybe she wears them to remind everybody in Benevolence of what happened to him. Folks can't help but think of Gus when they see his clothes coming their way. It doesn't matter that it's Delia who is wearing them. Those clothes, Gus's clothes, will keep right on reminding the men that killed him of what they did. That's what she's probably hoping.

And maybe it does remind them. Because I know I will never be able to look at Delia again without seeing Gus too.

The next day I am standing in the cafeteria line with Rayanne and Jinny when Chase struts in with that walk he's got. Very smooth. My heart picks up the pace, beating to his every step. Seems whenever Chase comes near me these days, I get a little wobbly in the knees.

He walks over to a table where a bunch of seniors are sitting, pulls out one of the chairs with his foot, spins it around, sits down facing the back, and rests his arms on the top. It's not even his lunch period. But that never stops Chase. For some reason, none of the teachers doing lunchroom duty ever seem to notice.

I know his routine. He never stands in line with everybody

else. If he is really hungry, he cuts in front of somebody. Nobody would ever dare challenge him. Otherwise, he waits till the line is gone, walks through, gets his food, and bolts it all down in two or three minutes.

Today he is waiting.

Last night was the first time in days that I didn't sneak out to be with him. I had a French test to study for. My grades in that class have taken a real nosedive. I haven't talked to Chase since I left school the day before. And the truth is, I've missed him.

I come through the line with my tray, knowing full well I have to be out of my mind for what I'm about to do, but I do it anyway. I tell Rayanne and Jinny I'll join them in a few minutes. Then I walk straight up to that table of seniors, look Chase square in the eyes and say, "Can I talk to you?"

Chase gives me that lazy grin of his. For a minute, I get the awful feeling he's going to leave me hanging. But then he stands up and jerks his thumb toward the empty table by the door. Nobody ever sits there because the legs are uneven and the table wobbles. Every kid in the cafeteria is watching us. I can feel their eyes boring into me. From the table over by the window, Willy and Earl are whooping and hollering and whistling like the complete morons they are. My face is burning with embarrassment. I wish like crazy that I'd thought this whole thing through a bit more before I went up to Chase's table.

I set my tray down. Chase slides into the chair next to mine. He helps himself to some of my meat loaf and sits there eating it with his fingers. "This is real cozy, Dove. Yep, you and me sitting here all alone with ten thousand kids gawking at us. I don't know why we didn't think of this before."

"I need to ask you something," I say, ignoring his sarcasm.

"Ask away."

"You hear anything about some trouble over at the migrant camp last week?"

"Like what?" He doesn't look at me.

"Well, I heard something. About some of our pickers. Seems some folks were over at the migrant camp last week and set their clothes on fire."

"Nobody was wearing those clothes, I hope," Chase says.

"I'm serious!"

"So am I."

"No," I tell him. "Just the clothes got burned. They were hanging on a clothesline."

He nods, like that's about what he was expecting me to say, then reaches for more meat loaf. The meat loaf usually tastes like roofing shingles, so I don't object. "Sounds to me like somebody's probably just trying to scare a few folks."

"You wouldn't happen to know who that somebody is, would you?"

"Why would you think I'd know anything about it?"

I nod in the direction of the table full of seniors he'd been sitting at. "I thought maybe you might have heard something."

Chase slides down in his chair and stretches his long legs out in front of him. "What's with all this sudden interest in the pickers?"

Jinny and Rayanne are watching Chase and me from

across the room. Jinny is smiling. Rayanne is not. Jinny starts to giggle, and Rayanne gives her a little smack on the shoulder.

Chase is watching them too. "You didn't ask me over here just to talk about what happened at the camp, now, did you?"

I tap my fork up and down on the mashed potatoes. I can't bring myself to eat them. They taste like the paste we used to use in grammar school. "Why else would I ask you over here?"

"Oh, I don't know. Maybe to announce to everybody in the school that we're a couple?"

Are we a couple? I want to ask. But I don't dare. Not here. When I don't say anything, Chase stands up and hooks his thumbs on the pockets of his dungarees. He tips his chin toward the cafeteria line, which has dwindled to two people. "You gonna be here when I get back?"

"You didn't answer my question yet. Do you know who did it? Or why?"

"You're something else, you know that?" He shakes his head and stares up at the ceiling. "Okay. Here's what I think. I wouldn't put it past some folks around here to use those rumors about your barn and those other fires to stir up trouble for the pickers."

"Our barn? What folks? Why?" I stand up with my half-empty tray. All I've managed to eat is the little square of spice cake, which suddenly reminds me of Rosemary Howell. I follow Chase over to the line, dropping off my tray on the way.

"Forget it, Dove," he says. "Whatever's going on, it's nothing you can do anything about."

I can tell by the look on his face that he considers this

conversation over. I leave him standing there in line and head off to French class. Part of me is furious that he wouldn't answer my questions, because I'm pretty sure he knows more than he's telling. And part of me is tickled to death that he called us a couple.

· · · · · · · · · · · · · · · · ·

It is too hot to sleep. The window fan makes scraping sounds, like someone is shoveling gravel at lightning speed. Mosquitoes the size of bald eagles are maneuvering their way through a hole in one of the screens. I turn on the light and dig through my desk drawer, looking for Scotch tape to patch the hole. No tape. I stuff a piece of tissue in the hole instead.

I've pretty much given up on Chase coming by tonight. I keep going over everything that happened in the cafeteria earlier wondering if I did something wrong. Maybe he doesn't want the whole school to know we're a couple yet. Maybe he doesn't even want us to be a couple. Maybe he doesn't think of me that way. Maybe he just likes making out with me in secret. This is what I'm stewing about when from somewhere below my window comes the snap of a branch, loud enough for me to hear it over the fan.

Someone or something is stomping around in the azalea bushes. The faint smell of cigarette smoke drifts in on the next wave of fanned air. I bolt upright in my bed. Sniff again to make sure. It is definitely cigarette smoke.

I fly out of bed and pull on my shorts and a blouse. I don't bother with shoes. I tiptoe past Dad's door. But this is wasted

127

effort. His door is wide open. His bed is still made up. He's not home yet. It's late, probably past midnight. And I have no idea where he is.

I head down the stairs, banging the screen door on my way out.

Chase is sitting beneath the oak outside my bedroom window. His back is pressed against the bark. He looks up.

"What are you doing here this late?" I ask.

He gets to his feet and stretches. "Same thing I've been doing almost every night for the past two weeks. Coming to see you."

"Most people who want to see each other go out on a date. A *date*. Ever hear of it?" I've been meaning to bring this up in a more subtle way, when the time is right. But there it was—it just came tumbling right out of my mouth.

Chase grins at me. "So, consider this a date, then."

"It's after midnight," I tell him. "How come you waited till now to come over?"

Chase crushes his cigarette with the toe of his boot. "Lost track of time, I guess."

Overhead the moon is full. It sets the shiny leaves in the groves to shimmering. I start walking toward them. Chase comes up behind me. He does a few circles around me, bouncing on the balls of his feet. "Oh, come on, Dove," he says. "I was joking about this being a date. You want to go on a date? Okay, how about Saturday night? We'll go to a movie."

There is something about being in the groves at this hour with the moonlight peeking in and out of hazy clouds that sets my blood to dancing under my skin. Mosquitoes buzz in my ears. I brush them away and take off running. I dart in and around the orange trees where the moonlight can't reach. I am daring Chase to come after me. Like when we used to play hide-and-seek as kids.

I hear the soft thud of his footsteps behind me. He is laughing. And I start laughing too. I get down on my knees to climb under one of the trees. Chase is right behind me. We crawl under one, then over to another. We are acting like six-year-olds. I feel light and free.

I try to scoot from beneath the tree, but Chase clamps his hand on my ankle, keeping me from crawling any farther. He holds both my legs while he gently slides me back under the glossy branches. The scent of orange blossoms makes me dizzy. He is beside me on the ground.

"Dove," he whispers in my ear, "this is my formal invitation. Will you do me the honor of accompanying me to the movies Saturday night?" His hand, gliding along my side, is like wind on my body. I could lie here forever, feeling his soft touch.

We stay that way for a long time. At one point I hear my dad's truck pulling around to the back of the house. But I don't move. He doesn't usually check on me when he gets home late. Not like he used to when I was little. I'm counting on that now.

I rub my face on Chase's T-shirt, taking in his scent. Something salty and sweet, mixed with orange blossoms. It makes me think about what Delia told me about Gus's sweater.

"You ever wonder who killed Gus Washburn?" I ask him.

Chase is lying next to me, looking up at the branches.

"What made you think of old Gus?" His voice is barely a whisper.

Even in the dark I can sense he's uneasy. "Delia told me what happened. How Cholly Blue saw the whole thing, thought he recognized one of the men in the car. But Cholly didn't have any proof, except his word. You know how it is."

"Yeah."

We don't say anything for a while. Then I feel Chase's warm hand slip into mine. "If I tell you something, you have to swear not to tell anybody," he says.

I don't like swearing to things I might not want to keep secret, and I tell him as much. Chase just lies there, quiet, like he's thinking. "It's about Gus," he says. "About the hit-and-run."

I roll onto my side. My face is only a few inches from his. I can barely make out his profile it's so dark under here. "Tell me."

"You have to swear."

"Okay," I say, finally.

"Say it."

"Okay. I swear."

Chase sits up as far as he can under the tree branches and lights a cigarette. "This one night, a few years back—I think it was the night after Gus died—I overheard Travis telling my dad about this accident. They were in our kitchen. Travis said he'd been drinking and lost control of the car and hit somebody. He said he thought it might have been Gus Washburn he hit, but he couldn't be sure. My dad told Travis it was best to keep quiet about it. That it'd blow over."

It takes a few seconds for what Chase has said to sink in.

Then it comes to me like a rush of ice-cold air when you open a freezer door. "Travis Waite was driving that car?"

"If you can call it that."

"And your dad knows?"

Chase stares down at the glowing tip of his cigarette. "So does yours. I'm pretty sure Travis told them both."

I sit up, hunch over, and grab my knees. The sickly sweet smell of rotting oranges—fruit that has fallen from the tree—seeps into my nostrils. It penetrates my pores. It is everywhere. My stomach is churning like an old washing machine. "But it wasn't Travis's pickup that hit Gus. That's all Travis has got, that old Ford pickup. The one with that stupid skunk tail on the antenna. Cholly Blue said it was a sedan."

Chase buries the cigarette in the sand and lies down next to me on his side. "They were driving some woman's car. Travis and Jimmy, they—"

"Jimmy Wheeler?" I lean toward him, tightening my grip on my knees. "Jimmy was in that car?"

"Yeah."

The rotten-orange smell has become liquid. It rises in my throat. I swallow hard, forcing it back down. No wonder Cholly Blue couldn't get anybody on the police force to follow up on Gus's murder, Jimmy being one of the local cops and all. It was Jimmy who'd been in the passenger seat that night. *That* was who Cholly had seen.

"Why would Travis tell your dad and mine about this? Why would he tell *anybody*?"

"Cholly Blue went to the police. He said he saw Jimmy in the car. I don't know for sure, but Jimmy probably told Spudder Rhodes what happened and Spudder told my dad. Best I can figure, my dad asked Travis flat out what happened that night. Lucas probably did too. They've all known each other since grammar school, Dove. You know how it is around here."

Chase is watching me. When I don't say anything, he starts in again. "The way Travis told it, they were having a few beers over at O'Malley's. And they met this woman who was already pretty drunk. I guess they thought if they drove her home. . . . Anyway, they put her in the backseat of her car and took off. They figured they'd take a shortcut through the colored quarters. Maybe stir up some trouble while they were at it. Travis said they were just having a little fun. They weren't fixing to kill anybody. He didn't mean for it to happen."

"But they *did* kill somebody," I say.

"Travis said it was an accident, Dove."

"No. It was *not* an accident, Chase Tully. If it was an accident, then they wouldn't have kept it secret all this time. They wouldn't have covered for him. Travis would have gotten charged with reckless driving or involuntary manslaughter or something. He would have maybe lost his license for a while. But it would have gone on record as an accident and everybody would have known how it happened and who was driving. That is how it works. A hit-and-run is a crime. It's leaving the scene of an accident. People can go to jail for that. And if it was on purpose—"

"It wasn't," Chase says.

I ignore this. "On *purpose*, like Cholly Blue said it was, it's called murder."

Chase lights another cigarette, and in the glow from his lighter I can tell by the look on his face that he knows I'm right. And this isn't something he's just figured out.

We sit there not saying anything for a few minutes. The smoke from Chase's cigarette stings my eyes, making them water. Then I say, "So how come your dad never told the county sheriff or the state police?" I am wondering the same thing about my own.

Chase lets out a heavy sigh. "My dad said he wasn't about to lose a good crew boss just because Travis was too drunk to pay attention to where he was going." Then he adds, "And neither was yours."

"Why didn't *you* go to the police, then?"

"Because my dad caught me listening that night. He beat the crap out of me for spying on him and Travis. That's what he called it, *spying*. He said if I ever told anybody what I heard, he'd have my hide tied to the back of his truck and dragged along Route Eighty-six. That's why."

I don't doubt Chase for a minute. I know what Jacob's temper is like. I've seen it in action. One time, when Chase was in third grade, Jacob messed up Chase's shoulder real bad. And even though everybody said it was an accident, including Chase himself, I know better. I was standing right there when Jacob caught us playing on the tractor and yanked Chase off the seat so hard, he dislocated his shoulder.

Sweat trickles down my neck and face. It is suffocating under this tree. Huge orange-tasting waves are slamming against the inside of my stomach. I crawl out from under the tree just in time to throw up every last bit of the fried chicken I had for dinner.

"Oh, God, Dove. You okay?" Chase crawls up behind me and puts his hand on my forehead. I shove him away.

I can't talk to him right now. All I want to do is get home. I stagger to my feet and take off running.

"Hey! Dove! You okay? Come on back here. Dove! Come on. Don't do this. Okay?"

I am afraid Chase will try to come after me, but he doesn't. After a while his voice trails off.

I keep on running. I run like Gator did that day of the storm. I run like the devil is on my heels.

For a while I sit in an old wicker rocker on the back porch. I can't bring myself to go in the house just yet. When I was little, Delia used to rock me in this same chair. Sometimes she would be reading and I'd climb into her lap. She would start reading out loud from wherever she was in her book. I remember this one August night—I must have been about seven—we were all about dying from the heat. Delia was sitting in the rocker, trying to read by the porch light. My dad was off somewhere, and Delia stayed late to baby-sit.

I remember settling myself in her lap and listening to her read this story about a lady, Miss Emily, who poisons her fiancé and then keeps his body locked in her upstairs bedroom.

Nobody ever finds out about it until she is dead and buried. Then the whole town—they'd been waiting like kids for Christmas to get a peek inside her house—finally goes inside and what they find is this skeleton in her bed.

Well, I almost died when Delia got to that last page. I was only seven, for heaven's sake.

I remember that night being so hot and humid and our clothes so damp that it felt like Delia and I were stuck together. And I remember the sound of the moths bumping against the porch light, and Delia taking up her glass of iced tea and circling my sweaty face with it. I can still feel that wet chill sliding across my forehead and down my cheeks.

Delia thought the story was funny. She said most folks usually had some kind of skeletons—meaning dark secrets—hidden someplace in their houses, and Miss Emily was more the rule than the exception. I didn't think much about that at the time. But ever since, whenever I find out something upsetting about a person I thought I knew, Miss Emily and her skeleton come popping into my head.

The moon is half hidden behind dark clouds now, and only a few streaks of light break through, cutting a glimmering path that reaches from heaven to the center of our groves. The scent of the Valencia blossoms hangs heavy in the still air. But it can't replace the odor of rotten oranges. The smell is all over me.

Not more than fifty yards away is the blackened shell of our old barn, the one my great-granddaddy Alderman built. In my mind I see that streak of lightning all over again. Hear the loud crack, louder than any gunshot, as the bolt hits the tip of the barn roof and skids down the side.

Maybe it was a judgment on my dad, that bolt of lightning, for keeping what he knew about Gus's murder to himself all these years.

I sit there on the porch till the mosquitoes get so bad I can't stand it another minute. Then I go inside. I tiptoe past Dad's door. He is snoring softly.

For a long while I sit at my desk, staring out the window. I can't seem to get my mind wrapped around Travis's killing Gus, and around the people who know about it but haven't done anything. Like my dad. How could he live with such a horrible secret all these years? How could he let Travis Waite go on working for him? How he could go on acting like normal whenever he's around Delia?

And that makes me wonder what else I don't know about my father.

The worst part is that I don't know how to make any of this right. There is no point in going to the police. Spudder and the others already know what happened. Or they know Travis's version, anyway. And then there's my promise to Chase not to say anything, which I wish to heaven I'd never made.

A streak of orange appears above the trees in the east. It looks as if somebody is slowly lifting a huge dark shade to let in the light. Only I can't bring myself to look at such a hopeful sight. I climb into bed without bothering to take off my dirty clothes and pull the covers up over my head.

• • • • • • • • • • • • • • • • •

I am out the door, heading for the school bus stop at the bottom of our dirt driveway before Delia or Dad even knows

I'm gone. I keep my back turned to the house. If I look around, I'm sure I'll see Delia standing on the front porch, spatula in hand, trying to get my attention. She hates it when I miss breakfast. Sure enough, her voice echoes down to me. But there is almost a quarter mile between us. I pretend I don't hear her calling.

My eyes are practically swollen shut from crying half the night. I am wearing sunglasses. My plan is to wear them all day. I don't talk to anybody on the bus that morning. Even though my sunglasses have set off a barrage of stupid jokes, like, "Who do you think you are, Audrey Hepburn?" "Maybe she thinks she's incognito." "Nah, she's probably a spy for the Soviets." Really dumb.

I ignore them. I ignore everybody.

I go late to homeroom so I don't have to talk to Rayanne. She stares at me the whole time, trying to get my attention. But I don't look her way. Mrs. Hatch asks me to please remove my glasses. I tell her I have special drops in my eyes that make them sensitive to light. She actually falls for this. I use the same excuse in Mr. Weaver's geometry class, and again in Mrs. Myers's history class. My plan is to skip lunch period so I don't have to see Rayanne or Jinny or anyone else.

The news going around the halls this morning is about a fire in Buford Radcliff's basement last night. It happened not long after he got home from sweeping floors at the movie theater. Everybody in town knows Buford's got so much junk in his basement he's barely got walking space. He even keeps piles of old newspapers dating back to before World War II down there. So I more or less dismiss the idea of somebody intentionally trying to find his way into Buford's basement for the sole purpose of setting fire to it, seeing as how I can't imagine anyone in their right mind wanting to do that. More than likely, Buford accidentally set it himself. Fortunately the fire department got there before the flames made it up the basement stairs. So Buford has still got his house, just not as many newspapers as he used to have.

Even though this fire, like all the others, was an accident, most of the kids are saying the pickers are behind it. A lot of their parents believe that too. They are scared out of their wits that there's going to be some kind of uprising and everybody is going to get their roofs set on fire right over their heads some night while they're sleeping. I can't for the life of me figure out why some folks are so anxious to believe something so stupid.

Chase hasn't been around all morning. He probably overslept, considering how late he was out last night. I would have stayed home myself, except then I'd have to face my dad and Delia. And I'm not ready to do that.

Right now I've got Chase all mixed up in my mind with Gus and Travis. Here, all this time, I thought I knew everything there was to know about Chase Tully. He's done some bad things over the years, like stealing that model plane from Woolworth's. But keeping a murder a secret? And then making me swear not to tell anybody? He brought me into this so he could ease his own conscience. I don't doubt that for a minute.

In English class I give Miss Poyer the eyedrops story. She looks up at me from the attendance book lying open on her desk. Her dark hair is piled loosely on top of her head. Renegade strands have escaped down her neck and the sides of her face. She's wearing big gold hoop earrings.

"Eyedrops?" She tips her head to the side. A slow smile eases across her face. She doesn't buy my story, I can tell. But she doesn't ask me to remove the sunglasses, either.

We are studying the Beat poets, and this morning she is handing out copies of a book of poems by Lawrence Ferlinghetti. Miss Poyer is wearing a black skirt, black tights, and a dark purple blouse, which makes me wonder if maybe she is a Beat poet too. She doesn't dress like any of the other teachers.

We were supposed to read *Howl* by Allen Ginsberg, but all the parents got together and raised a ruckus. They said it was obscene. The next day the school board banned it. Naturally I can't wait to get my hands on a copy. Miss Poyer says it's brilliant. The jury is still out on Ferlinghetti's book, *A Coney Island of the Mind,* which is why Miss Poyer is handing out copies to everybody in class this morning and telling us to read it by Monday. I don't think any of the parents have had a chance to read it yet. Miss Poyer is going to try to outmaneuver them this time. I flip through the book during class. The school board is going to ban it all right. No question about it.

I plan to read the whole thing this weekend, like she asked, because they'll be in our classroom come Monday going up and down the aisles with an empty box asking us to deposit Ferlinghetti's book in it. That's what they did with Aldous Huxley's *Brave New World* last year. That happened in Miss Poyer's junior class. But everybody in the school heard about it. If she keeps this up, I doubt she'll be teaching at Benevolence High much longer. That would be too bad. Miss Poyer is the best teacher I've ever had.

I slip into the girls' room during lunch period. I don't stop by my locker, so I'm still carrying my geometry and history books and Ferlinghetti's poems.

Everyone is either in class or at lunch. I'm alone in the girls' room. Or at least I thought I was until I hear muffled sniffling sounds coming from the end stall. The door is closed. I bend down and spot dirty saddle shoes. I know these shoes. A frayed blue loose-leaf binder lies on the floor next to them.

I knock softly on the stall door. "Rosemary?"

Sniff.

"Are you okay?"

No answer.

"It's Dove."

Two more sniffs. The sound of toilet paper being pulled from the roll. Snuffling snorts. Lots of nose blowing.

"I'm fine," she says. It comes out like half a sob.

"That's why you're spending your lunch period in that stall, because you're fine?" Considering my own reasons for being here, I don't have any right to form an opinion on Rosemary's hiding place of choice.

I hear the sound of more toilet paper unwinding. More nose blowing.

"Nobody else is out here," I tell her. "It's just me."

The stall door opens a few inches. Rosemary stands there with eyes that match mine. I wish I had another pair of sunglasses to loan her.

"Willy and Earl?" I ask.

She nods. "I can't go to chem class looking like this," she says. "Willy's in that class."

I've had about as much of school as I can take for one day.

My mind has been all tied up with what happened the night before. I don't remember a single thing that went on in my classes this morning. This isn't likely to change anytime soon. Certainly not in time for French class.

"Let's get out of here, okay?" I say.

Rosemary wipes the wad of toilet paper across each puffy eye. "Leave? School, you mean?"

I take off my sunglasses. Rosemary stares at my face for a few seconds, then says, "Okay." She picks up her frayed binder.

We have to move fast. The bell is going to ring in about five minutes. Slipping through the front door is definitely out. We would have to go by the main office. We decide on the side door near the gym. It leads to the parking lot. The plan is to hunker down and wind our way between cars, hoping no one will see us if they look out the classroom windows. On the other side of the parking lot are some woods. I have no idea what we will do when we get there. I haven't thought that far ahead.

By the time we make it to the woods, Rosemary is actually giggling. She's enjoying this. It brings a little smile to my face too.

"Now what?" She looks at me. Expectation and hope are beaming all over her face. I am her leader. Her savior. And suddenly I wish I'd never knocked on that bathroom stall door.

"We can't go anywhere public. Anybody who sees us will know we're skipping school."

Rosemary agrees. She is still waiting for me to tell her what to do next. I stare down at the books in my arms. Ferlinghetti's book is on top.

"There's an old cemetery on the other side of the woods. A cemetery for colored folks. I found it once, years ago when I was supposed to be running laps in gym," I tell her. "It's near a cypress swamp. Nobody will find us there." No white people, anyway. But I don't say this out loud.

Rosemary follows me through the thick brush along a path that is almost fully overgrown. No one has come this way in a long time. I hear her slapping at mosquitoes behind me, but she doesn't say anything. By the time we come to the open clearing, my stockings are in shreds and we are both covered with stinging sandspurs. I set my books on the ground by a headstone that looks as if it's been stained with tobacco juice and unhook my stockings from my garter belt. I roll them down, kick off my flats, and pull off the ruined stockings.

Rosemary seems amused by this. "I hate wearing those things," she says, picking sandspurs from her socks. "Well now, will you look at that." She points to a wooden cross not far from an old shed. A little teddy bear, made out of faded blue-checked gingham, rests against the cross.

I look around. It is like this everywhere in the cemetery— little treasures left next to the tombstones: a chipped bowl filled with seashells, plastic pop beads looped over a headstone, a dirt-crusted Coke bottle stuffed with plastic geraniums. Photographs encased in glass rest against the base of some of the headstones. Some are even embedded right in the tombstone. Most of the headstones have names and dates. But a few of the really old stones have only initials carved on them. Some aren't anything more than brown stones, no names, no initials. There don't seem to be many epitaphs here.

I come across the grave of a boy named Curtis B.

Washington. 1920–1935. Curtis is my age. I sit down next to his grave and open Ferlinghetti. It *is* Friday, so it only seems natural to stick with my routine.

Rosemary doesn't even ask what I'm doing. She sits down across from me. I tell her about reading poems—mostly love poems—to dead boys in cemeteries. Rosemary smiles. "That's real nice of you," she says. She acts as if this is something folks do every day, like brushing their teeth or changing their underwear. I'm beginning to like Rosemary.

I flip through the pages, sliding my index finger over the lines, waiting for it to find the word *love*. My finger stops its journey on poem number 25. Apparently Emily Dickinson isn't the only poet who doesn't bother with titles. "Okay," I tell Rosemary. "Here's one."

I read this poem about the heart gasping like "a foolish fish." About halfway through I realize this isn't a love poem. It's about the heart in love, dying alone and unnoticed.

When I'm finished, Rosemary shifts a few times and rearranges her crinolines and skirt. "Well, at least poor Curtis won't feel like he's missing out on anything." She runs her fingers over the chiseled letters of Curtis B. Washington's name. Then she asks to see the book I'm reading from. I hand it over to her. She flips through the pages.

"Gator and me, we sometimes meet at the Baptist cemetery," she says. She doesn't look up from the book. "We go for walks in the woods behind the church."

I don't move a muscle. I don't even blink. I'm thinking about how Rosemary just suddenly showed up at the Baptist cemetery that day I was reading epitaphs to Gator.

"How'd you happen to meet him?" I ask. "I mean, you said your folks don't live at the migrant camp."

Rosemary keeps flipping through the pages of my book. Finally she says, "At the Gulf station. First day we got here. Daddy stopped to fill up the truck. We had the trailer hitched up to it. I got out to use the bathroom—our trailer doesn't have one—and sitting on the ground, leaning up against some old tires, was this colored boy. He was drawing something on a brown paper bag. He looked up at me when I walked by and he smiled. Well, I didn't know what to think, a colored boy smiling at me that way. But he's got a real friendly smile and such a nice face. Have you ever noticed that?"

I don't say anything. I'm still stuck back at the part where Rosemary told me she and Gator have been secretly meeting at the cemetery.

She doesn't seem to notice. She goes right on with her story. "So there I was, smiling right back without thinking."

Rosemary blushes. I pretend to be examining the pop beads looped over the headstone next to Curtis Washington's. I'm working hard to shove any thoughts of Rosemary and Gator being anything more than friends right out of my head. Because it is too disturbing to think about.

"Right about then our dog, Roose—that's short for Roosevelt—he leaped out of the pickup window—he'd been sitting in the front seat with Daddy and my brother, Charlie—and just like that he took off like a bat out of hell," Rosemary says. "Charlie hightailed it after him, but Roose was on a tearing streak. Guess he'd been cooped up in the truck too long."

Rosemary stretches her legs out in front of her. She crosses them at the ankles and leans back on her elbows.

"Well, he spun himself in circles, all of us chasing and calling after him, dumb mutt, when suddenly he just stops. He's panting and slobbering. And we're calling to him to come on and get in the truck. But instead he walks over to Gator and licks him on the face, like they're old friends who haven't seen each other in years. Gator rubs him behind the ears, and Roose about tumbles into his lap, he's so happy.

"Charlie and Daddy, they don't have any idea what to do next. Daddy starts yelling at Charlie for letting the dog out, and Charlie is yelling back that the dog let himself out. And Ma comes out of the trailer with Biddy on her hip—Biddy's my baby sister—yelling about all the yelling. Gator, he just sits there rubbing Roose's ears and watching us like we're the best show in town."

Rosemary sits up and brushes off her elbows.

"While all the yelling was going on, I went over, got Roose, and put him back in the truck. I thanked the boy, though. He said, 'I didn't do anything but sit here.' I said, 'Well, I guess that was enough.' And he told me his name was Gator. I didn't see him again until—" Rosemary's body seems to cave in on itself.

"That Saturday across from the movie theater?" I ask. "When Willy and Earl showed up?" The minute the words are out of my mouth, I regret it. I don't want to remember that day. And I'm pretty sure Rosemary doesn't want to either. Her face is turning bright red.

"No. Before that." She gets to her feet and brushes off her skirt. "I've got to get to Luellen's, or she'll have a fit."

I look down at my watch. It's almost three.

Up until now I thought the only times Rosemary talked to

Gator were that day outside of Tuckett's Hardware and the day she ran into us in the Baptist cemetery. But I can see now that I was fooling myself. Pretending those were just coincidences. It's as plain as the nose on my face that Rosemary and Gator have been secretly seeing each other whenever they can. Maybe even sneaking out at night, like Chase and me.

Rosemary picks up her frayed binder. "This has been a real interesting way to spend an afternoon, reading poems to dead folks," she says over her shoulder as she's walking away.

I want to ask her what it is about Gator that makes her face turn the color of strawberries. I want to ask her if she's completely out of her mind, considering there are plenty of people like Willy and Earl ready to pound her and Gator into dust for flaunting the rules in their faces.

I also want to ask her if she knows anything about Travis Waite cheating the pickers, seeing as how she knew about the clothesline fire. But she is already halfway across the cemetery. My questions hang there like little clouds in the sticky air.

It is after seven when I get home. I wanted to make sure dinner would be over and Delia had left for the day. In the oven I find a pie tin with two thick pork chops, a sweet potato, turnip greens, and a warm biscuit. Delia's doing. Everything is swimming in gravy just the way I like it. I set the pie tin on the table, not bothering to transfer the food to a regular plate. As I'm rummaging around in the silverware drawer, I get an eerie feeling. The back of my neck tingles. I am not alone.

I don't turn around. I stand stock-still, clenching my fork and knife in one hand.

"Where you been?" Dad says.

"With a friend from school."

"You're late."

"Lost track of time," I tell him.

"Dinner's at five-thirty. Since when do you come waltzing in here after seven?"

"Since tonight." I still have my back to him.

"We eat at the same time in this house."

I don't know how to tell him that I don't think I could sit at the same table with him anymore. Knowing what I do about him covering up for Travis, I can hardly bring myself to look at his face.

"Look at me when I'm talking to you," he says.

I walk over to the pie tin, pick it up, and head for the front hall. I have to squeeze past him. He fills almost the whole doorway.

His hand lands on my shoulder. "You want to tell me what this is about?" His voice is softer now. He looks worried.

I don't answer. I slip away from his hand and make my way to the stairs. My dad and I have never been much for long conversations. I figure he'll get the message.

He does.

He looks away and shakes his head. Then he wanders off and leaves me be. I am hoping it will stay like this—the two of us going our separate ways, minding our own business, even though we are living under the same roof. Because I don't have anywhere else to go.

I take my dinner upstairs and set it on my desk. I haven't eaten a thing since last night. Right now I'm starved. I wolf down the food as if it's my last meal.

Ever since I found out about Travis killing Gus, I have been trying to think what to do. Delia has a right to know what happened. But if I tell her, she will probably quit working for us, and I can't bear the thought of her leaving. Delia has been here my whole life. It would be worse than losing my mom because I don't remember my mother all that well.

From below I hear the roar of Dad's truck coming to life. He's going out somewhere again. Seems like he's been going out a lot more than usual lately. I wipe a few drops of gravy from my chin.

I finish reading all of the Ferlinghetti poems even though I have the whole weekend ahead of me.

* * * * * * * * * * * * * * * * *

It is a hot night, too hot to be in my stuffy bedroom. I am about to settle in on the front porch swing with an extra pillow, my transistor radio, and a glass of iced tea, wearing nothing but my light bathrobe over my baby-doll pajamas, when here comes Chase, tearing up the dirt road in his T-bird with the top down and dust flying all over the place. He circles into our driveway and stops right in front of the porch steps. He sits there grinning at me for a few seconds. Without bothering to open the car door, he slides up onto the back of the seat, swings his legs over the side, and lifts himself up. He takes our porch steps in two leaps and lands next to me on the swing, which about jars the teeth right out of my skull.

He fingers the lace ruffle on my robe and grins. "Looks like you were expecting me." His hand travels down my arm. It's like soft waves washing over my skin and spreading through my whole body.

"You weren't in school today," I say.

Chase leans back in the swing, crossing his long legs at the ankles and making himself right at home. "So? I'm not in school a lot of days."

I have no idea what I was expecting him to say. Even if what happened in the groves last night upset him as much as it did me, he'd never let on.

Chase presses his heels to the floor and begins rocking the swing back and forth. We don't talk for a while. We float gently on the swing, listening to the Platters singing "Smoke Gets in Your Eyes."

Suddenly I'm wondering if Rosemary and Gator are somewhere listening to a radio too. I look over at Chase. "If I tell you something, will you swear not to tell?" I figure he owes me one.

Chase just frowns. "Tell me what?"

"Swear," I say.

"Fine. Consider me sworn."

"What would you say if I told you Gator has a white girl-friend?"

Chase stares at me for a few seconds, thinking. "I'd say he wasn't planning to live very long."

I nod. This was more or less what I'd expected him to say—expected anybody in this town to say.

"Things are going to get pretty bad for him and the other pickers as it is without him doing something stupid like that. It's just going to rile folks up even more."

"Bad for Gator and the pickers? Why?" I remember what Chase told me at lunch yesterday, about folks trying to scare the pickers. "Is someone planning to set fire to more clotheslines over at the camp?"

He reaches for my glass of iced tea and helps himself to a healthy swallow. "You're a lousy hostess, Dove, you know that?"

"Well, are they?"

"There's talk, that's all. Some folks around here are worried about those fires."

"What folks?" An uneasy feeling has started to creep over me, setting my skin to prickling.

Chase presses his heels to the floor and begins rocking the swing again. He doesn't say anything.

"Is it because of those rumors about our barn?"

Chase shrugs, like he doesn't much care. And that scares me a little. "Could be part of it. Who knows?" he says.

I pull my knees up close to my chest, trying to cover my bare feet with my robe.

"But *nobody* burned our barn," I say, my voice rising a notch. "How many times do I have to keep saying that? It was lightning. Your dad, Spudder, Moss, Jimmy, they were all there. They *know* it was lightning." A moth bumps against my cheek. I swat it away. "You told them, right? You told them Willy made up that stupid story, didn't you?"

"It's like you said, they were there. I didn't have to tell them anything."

"Then why would anybody act like they believe one of the pickers did it? Why would they want to cause trouble for them?"

Chase takes a deep breath. He works at his face, trying to look patient. "They just do, okay?"

"It's *not* okay," I tell him. "There's got to be a reason."

"It's complicated," he says. As if that explained everything.

My head is spinning. Near as I can figure, there are people in this town *pretending* to believe the rumors that are going around so they can use them as an excuse to hurt colored folks. But why? It doesn't make any sense.

My stomach is getting all queasy again. The last thing I need is to throw up in front of Chase two nights in a row. "I have to go in," I tell him. "My dad will have both our hides if he catches us out here, me dressed like this."

"Your dad isn't going to be home for hours," he says, downing the last of my iced tea.

"How would you know?"

"Because he's over at our place, along with a few of the boys."

"What boys?"

He looks down at the empty glass. "Travis and them."

I have a bad feeling about this. But I can't bring myself to ask him any more questions. I stand up and move toward the front door. "You better go now," I tell him. "I'm not feeling very well."

The look on Chase's face about breaks my heart. I can tell he was planning on spending the evening with me. And I don't know how to tell him that I've suddenly got these disturbing thoughts screaming in my head. Terrifying thoughts. Thoughts about my dad and all those nights he's been going out lately.

"You going to be okay for tomorrow night?" Chase is watching me. He looks worried.

I stare at him. I don't know what he's talking about.

"Our date. Remember?" He gives me a funny look, then comes across the porch and gently rests his hands on my shoulders. "You okay?"

"I'll be all right." I rest my cheek on his hand. Then I slip away and leave him there on the porch.

Inside I lock the door, turn off the porch light, then, one by one, all the lights in the house, leaving us both in the dark.

A few minutes later I look out the front window. Chase is still there. He's sitting on the top step with his shoulders hunched and his head in his hands. I know he's wondering why I didn't so much as kiss him good night. It about tears me apart, seeing him like that. But there is something I need to find out. Something I couldn't bring myself to tell him. Something that started as a tiny suspicion, nibbling away at me when Chase was talking about my dad being over at his house, a suspicion that has swelled into a question that fills my whole mind.

A short time later I hear his car heading out of the driveway. I turn all the lights back on and begin my search. The truth is, I'm not really sure what it is I'm looking for.

I start in the attic, opening every dusty old trunk. I dig through the toolboxes in the barn. I rummage through every drawer in the house. The last room I search is Dad's office. It would have made sense to begin here, but I was too scared. Dad's office has always been off-limits to me. Even Delia isn't allowed in here to clean. It's complete chaos, and my dad doesn't want anyone trying to tidy it up for him. He says he knows exactly where everything is. It's his own system. Which to my way of thinking is no system at all.

Piles of papers and magazines are everywhere—all these file folders, all these envelopes—it's a mess. This is why I didn't want to have to look in here. Too much stuff to go through.

I stand in the middle of the piles in my robe and pajamas, wondering where on earth to begin. Stacks of papers and envelopes hide the top of his desk. I decide to start with the desk drawers. I'm half expecting them to be locked. But the middle drawer opens right up. The tray along the front holds pencils and pens, erasers, and paper clips. In the corner is a stack of cards. The one on top looks like my dad's driver's license. I lift it up and see that's exactly what it is, an expired one. There are other cards, mostly expired. This doesn't surprise me. My dad doesn't like to throw anything out. He even has copies of his old high school newspapers in a stack on top of his filing cabinet.

I shuffle through the rest of the old cards, not really paying much attention, when suddenly I see something that cuts my breath right off. I am holding a blue-green card with the letters *KKK* at the top. And there, at the bottom, is my dad's signature.

Saturday night Chase and I go to the drive-in to see *Some Like It Hot*. I don't much care one way or the other if my dad finds out.

Chase doesn't appear to notice anything is wrong. I watch the movie. I laugh in all the right places, even though nothing seems funny. I eat popcorn. A few of the pieces stick in my throat. I let Chase kiss me. But the kisses don't feel the same. They don't feel like anything at all.

Everything has changed.

As we're coming back through town, Chase makes a sudden sharp turn down a side street. I have no idea where we're going, and I don't bother to ask. Chase makes another sharp turn. We are in the back alley behind the Benevolence Hotel. "Remember this?" he says.

I look to where Chase is pointing and see Amos Pritchett's old electric chair. Amos Pritchett owns the Benevolence Hotel. He also owns the only funeral home in town, which is right next door. Amos has been known to take out one ad in the *Benevolence Press* for both businesses. His latest slogan for the Benevolence Hotel and Funeral Home is "We offer comfortable lodgings for one night or all eternity." The best thing about the Benevolence Hotel, which doesn't have much else going for it except its Sunday brunches, is that electric chair. Nobody knows where Amos got it, but it still has all the electrodes and straps on it.

When we were little, Chase and I used to run over to the hotel after school. The elementary school is a lot closer to the center of town than the high school. We would sneak up on the porch to play with Amos's electric chair.

We used to take turns strapping each other in; then we'd give each other a chance to make a last-minute confession before we pulled the switch. Our only rule was that your confession had to be something real, not something you made up. It had to be something you wanted to get off your chest before you died. We played this game every chance we got, which is why Chase and I know a lot more about each other than most folks would care to.

Amos always caught us and chased us off, yelling loud enough for the whole town to hear. But that didn't stop us. We always came back.

Like now.

Chase stops the car and hops out of the T-bird, taking the

porch steps two at a time, and flops down in the electric chair. I follow right behind him. He reaches up and pulls me into his lap. "Let's make some electricity," he whispers in my ear.

It's been years since we played with Amos's electric chair. I'd almost forgotten about it.

Sitting in that old chair, even in Chase's lap, suddenly makes me uncomfortable. I stand up and put my hands on the porch railing. I am afraid he will try to get a confession out of me, like when we were kids. And I have secrets I don't want to tell—can't tell.

"You used to wangle a last-minute confession out of me before you threw the switch, remember?" Chase says.

I nod, but I don't turn around.

"I love you," he whispers to my back. "I always have."

He reaches for my hand. When I turn to look at him, Chase says, "You can pull the switch now."

* * * * * * * * * * * * * * * *

For the rest of the week I feel as if I am only going through the motions, pretending everything is fine. I avoid my dad whenever I can. Just looking at him makes me want to cry.

I take the notes Rayanne passes me in homeroom, scribble some stupid answer, and slip them back to her. I dutifully deposit my copy of *A Coney Island of the Mind* in the box Marilee Redfern, who is head of the school board, carries up and down the aisles between our desks in Miss Poyer's class. I don't even flinch when I toss it in with the rest of the banned copies.

I let Chase walk me to my classes. I do all the things I always do, but it feels as if I am outside of myself watching somebody else do them.

Even with Chase—even with him telling me he loved me that night on the back porch of the hotel—things aren't right. I know I should be thrilled to the bone. But what happened that night, it's like something I saw in a movie or on TV. It doesn't seem real.

All week I've been trying to understand why my dad would be a member of an organization that is known for hating just about everybody who isn't them. But no matter which way I turn it over in my head, I can't make it work. And I don't have the faintest idea what to do with this terrible knowledge.

When I was in eighth grade, my social studies teacher, Mr. Stone, spent one whole class period doing what he called "dispelling the evil myths about the Klan." He said people were wrong about the Ku Klux Klan scaring and hurting people. He told us they did a lot of good for the communities, like donating money to charities and bringing baskets of food to the poor, including colored folks. He even passed around this photograph of Klansmen dressed in their robes and hoods, handing a basket of food to a colored man at an old folks' home. Staring at that picture, all I could think was how those poor old colored people must have been scared out of their wits when those white robes came waltzing through the front door—food baskets or no food baskets.

Mr. Stone said the Klan even got General Robert E. Lee behind them. Mr. Stone seemed real proud of that fact. Although he admitted General Lee wanted his support to remain invisible, which, according to Mr. Stone, is how the Klan got nicknamed the Invisible Empire. The way I see it, if General Lee was ashamed to have his name associated with the Klan, except in secret, that doesn't speak well for the Klan.

Looking back, I can see Mr. Stone probably had reasons of his own for telling our class what he did. Maybe he even belonged to the Klan. Lord knows, he certainly spent a lot of time talking about Communism and how we had to be on the lookout for any suspicious folks who might be Communist spies, even our own neighbors.

But the picture I can't seem to get out of my head these days is the one Billy Tyler passed around in fifth grade, the picture of that poor colored man hanging from a tree.

So for now, anyway, I have stopped asking Delia and Chase and everyone else questions about the pickers. Because the truth is, I am afraid of the answers.

. . . .

On Friday night I am sitting at my desk, staring at my open geometry book, which doesn't seem to have anything to do with me. Monday's math test looms out there somewhere in space, a figment of Mr. Weaver's imagination. This is somebody else's life I've accidentally stumbled into. Time feels as if it's stretching and stretching, farther and farther—a rubber band that sooner or later is going to snap back and catch me in the face. But right now this math test doesn't seem real. Nothing does.

It is the roar of my dad's truck that finally pulls me back

into myself. I rush down the hall to the guest room window in time to see him heading down the dirt road to the highway.

My skin is prickling all over. I need to know what's going on. No matter how afraid I am of the answers.

I race down the stairs, grab a set of keys from the row of hooks by the phone, and head outside. The black pickup is still here. Dad took the red one. Without any plan beyond finding out where he's going, I climb into the driver's seat. My driver's permit is upstairs in my purse. It doesn't matter. I am not supposed to drive without an adult in the car anyway. Either way, I'm in trouble. But I don't much care.

The dust kicked up from the tires of Dad's pickup hasn't even settled yet. It drifts back into the open windows of the truck I am driving as I tear down the road after him. My skin buzzes with a kind of tingly electricity. Like a bat zeroing in on a mosquito, I home in on Dad's taillights, keeping enough distance between us that he won't recognize who is behind him.

I try to pay attention to where we're going because I'll have to find my way back home on my own. We pull off the county highway, go a few miles down a narrow road, then turn onto a dirt one. I know where we are. I have been coming to Fourth of July barbecues here ever since I can remember. We are heading straight for Spudder Rhodes's ranch house. I turn off the headlights, keeping only the parking lights on. I stay as far behind Dad as possible, hoping he can't see these dim lights in his rearview mirror. To my right is a small clearing. I pull the truck into it and park behind a thicket of saw palmetto. It probably isn't more than another five hundred yards to Spudder's house.

But when I sneak up to the front yard, there is not a single car, truck, or motorcycle in sight. Only the honking bullfrogs and the buzzing cicadas remind me that I'm not home in bed dreaming all this.

A light comes from the back of Spudder's house. I slip across the yard to the front bay window, where I stumble over the azalea bushes and scrape the dickens out of my legs. From here I can see through the dining room to the lighted kitchen. Spudder's wife, Nadine, is at the sink washing dishes. Or washing something, anyway. She has on bright green shorts. Her hair is wound in small wire rollers. Best I can tell, there is no one else around.

Across from Spudder's place, on the other side of the dirt road, is a meadow, and beyond that more woods, thick with oaks and pines. The moon is still bright enough for me to see that tire tracks have been cut through the grass in the meadow. I have never been on this side of Spudder's property. I'm not even sure it belongs to him. But I set off across the field, keeping to the ruts, until I get to the other side. I don't see anything but trees up ahead, not until I'm past the first few rows of dense woods and shrubs. Here the ruts suddenly bear sharply to the right, where I find another dirt road. It is hardly wide enough for a truck to get through. I can tell it's been well traveled. The dirt is rock hard here.

The mosquitoes are bleeding me dry. I don't swat at them. I am afraid someone might hear the slapping sounds. My eyes sting from salty sweat. The air here is so heavy I have to struggle for each breath.

The moonlight doesn't reach this far into the woods. I can barely see my sneakers. It is all I can do to keep to the road.

Sweat streaks down my face. It runs from my armpits along my sides. But I keep moving forward.

A harsh glaring light suddenly bursts in front of me. I slip behind a saw palmetto, hunch down, and rub my eyes. I pray that it wasn't a flashlight someone was shining in my face.

In the distance I hear voices. I creep out of my hiding place and inch slowly up the road, which is now brightly lit, sticking close to the edge of the woods. And there, off to my left, attached to the top of an old telephone pole, is the biggest cross I have ever seen. Both sides of it are covered with white lightbulbs. This is where the glaring light is coming from. It's as if somebody has adjusted the moon to concentrate all of its light right in this one spot. I don't dare walk the rest of the way on this road. Somebody will spot me for sure.

I keep low, making my way through the shrubs. My shorts and blouse and socks are covered with sandspurs. They sting my arms and legs. I don't slow down. I keep following the light and the sound of voices.

When I get to the edge of an open meadow, I hunker down behind a rotting tree trunk. Across the way, next to the telephone pole with the cross, are a pale green cinder-block building and a silver trailer, side by side. There are so many cars and trucks that I can't even begin to count them all. They are parked in neat rows over to one side of the field.

I want to be dreaming. I don't want any of what is happening here to be real. Because I know in a heartbeat what this place is. This is where the Klan is meeting. Not in Alabama. Not in Mississippi. Not someplace else. It's meeting right here in Benevolence, Florida.

Some of the men are hanging around outside, smoking and talking, including Moss Henley and Jimmy Wheeler. This doesn't surprise me any. If Spudder's in the Klan, he's not going to want anybody working with him who doesn't see things his way. The door to the cinder-block building is open, but I can't tell what's going on inside. I don't see my dad, but I know he is here. Judging from the large crowd, it looks like something big is going to happen.

A light spills from the windows of the silver trailer. The door opens and Jacob Tully steps outside. Two other men follow behind him. One is my dad. Jacob turns around to say something to the other one. He puts his hand on the man's shoulder, then steps away. When he does, I find myself looking straight into the face of Chase Tully.

I dig my fingernails into the decomposing log. Bark flakes off in chunks. The exposed areas are soft, which surprises me. I bend my face close. The musty smell of decaying wood drifts up my nose. I close my eyes. Everything is buzzing and humming on different frequencies—cicadas, peepers, bullfrogs, mosquitoes, crickets—all screaming inside my head. The more I try to block out the noise, the louder the night sounds. But the voices of the men are winning. They drown out everything else. If I open my eyes, I will have to look at them. At Chase. At Dad.

I turn away and crawl along the ground behind the shrubs, keeping the dirt road in my line of vision. I don't look back. Sharp twigs gouge my palms and knees. I pick up more sandspurs along the way. But I don't stop to pull them off. Their sting helps me to focus.

When I am far enough from the blazing lightbulbs, I get

to my feet and run. I run until my lungs burn, until my stomach cramps. I run past Spudder Rhodes's house, which is now dark. Nadine has gone to bed. I wonder if she has pulled the covers up over her head. Does she know what is happening less than a half mile from her house? Does she care?

If I could I would keep on running forever. It isn't until I am almost to the end of Spudder's road that I remember I drove Dad's truck here.

19

I head back to get the truck and ten minutes later I am pounding on Luellen Sutter's apartment door. She stands there in a red satin robe, holding a comb. The hair on one side of her head is in rollers, the other side hangs wet and limp.

"Dove Alderman?" The way she says my name tells me just how crazy it must look, my showing up at her door at this hour of the night. Somebody she knows only as one of her customers. Somebody with gritty bark under her fingernails, dirt all over her hands and knees, sandspurs stuck to her clothes and hair, and sweat dripping off her a gallon a minute. That she doesn't slam the door in my face right on the spot is a tribute to her good manners.

"I'm real sorry, Luellen, bothering you like this, at this hour. But I need to talk to Rosemary."

Luellen takes a step back. "Well, sure, then. Course you can. Come on in." She points the comb in the direction of the kitchen table. Rosemary looks up at me from where she sits, surrounded by open books, writing something in her loose-leaf binder. She takes one look at me and is on her feet in a flash.

"Did something happen?" She takes me by the arm, steers me into a chair at the kitchen table, and gets a bottle of RC Cola from the fridge. Luellen hasn't moved from her post at the front door. She is probably hoping this will only take a minute or two and I'll be heading out.

While Rosemary, wearing an oven mitt for protection, plucks sandspurs out of my hair and off my clothes, I tell her I have a bad feeling that something is going to happen to some of the pickers. If not tonight, then sometime over the weekend.

She doesn't ask me how I know this. But Luellen does.

I shake my head. Soda fizzes up my nose. I can barely swallow it. "I just do, okay?"

Luellen backs off. She closes the front door. I guess she's figured out I'm not leaving anytime soon.

* * * * * * * * * * * * * * * * *

I ask Rosemary to drive Dad's pickup. It will go better for both of us if we are caught. At least she has her license. Right now I'm not sure my mind would be on my driving, anyway. And Rosemary knows how to get to the migrant camp.

On the way she tells me how Travis Waite transported a busload of Mexicans across the border into Texas last fall and then brought them to Florida. "He said he would pay their way and they could pay him back. Except most of them don't speak English," Rosemary says. "Travis, he tells them they can get credit at the camp store, which he owns along with the camp. He's going to set them up just fine. Uh-huh." Rosemary shakes her head, looking disgusted. "Only, when it comes time to pay them, he says their wages have to go to paying off their debts. He keeps the money. They never see a cent.

"Besides what they owe him for bringing them here, he's charging them even more than he charges the other pickers for rent and food, which is already way too much. The Mexicans, though, they don't know the difference. The other pickers know what's going on, but they don't have much choice but to take what they get.

"Gator tried to explain it to the Mexican pickers. He told them Travis has been cheating everybody for years. Not just them, the Mexicans. If Travis gets fifty cents for each box the workers pick, he maybe gives them ten or twelve cents. Keeps most of it himself. The other crew leaders aren't much better, and some are a lot worse. Doesn't matter whether they're white or colored. Some of the colored crew bosses cheat their own kind too. They figure if that's how white folks do business, then that's just how it's done."

"Gator—has he been trying to do something about Travis cheating the pickers?" I ask her.

Rosemary misses her turn. She hits the brake and backs up the truck a few feet. She tugs at the steering wheel to get us back on course.

"He's been talking to some of them is all."

"*Just* talking?"

She turns on the high beams. She doesn't answer me. The moon has been swallowed up by dark clouds. The night is as thick as tar out here. We don't talk the rest of the way.

The camp is about two miles outside of Benevolence, heading northeast. It is tucked back in an open field just off the highway. Two dull, moth-cluttered spotlights shine down from a pole, spreading their dim light over the camp.

On one side of a wide dirt road stands a row of long build-ings with alternating doors and windows that puts me in mind of a barracks or a shabby motel. Even in this dim light I can see most of the paint has flaked away over the years. The tin roofs are crusted with rust. Across the way sits a bunch of small shacks. A few still have a light on inside. Some have one front door with tiny screenless windows on either side. Some just have a door. The sides are wood, with poles propping open tin flaps to let in air. Like the row buildings, they have rusty tin roofs and sit on wooden posts a few feet above the ground.

Clotheslines stretch between the shacks, weighted down with soggy faded shirts and dungarees. Women's underpants and bras—gray and worn—hang limp from some of the lines. I think what it must have been like the night those men came through here and set one of the clotheslines on fire. I know how scared I was the night the lightning hit our barn, and how sad and empty I felt later.

Everywhere I look, rusted oil drums overflow with garbage. Some lie on their sides. Knocked over by dogs more than likely, or raccoons. I see something darting around one of the piles, its long wormlike tail writhing as it noses through the trash. I spot another, and another. Rats. Dozens of them. My stomach does a little flip and I look away.

At the end of the road is a larger building. Unlike the other buildings, this one has a porch. Although it isn't anything more than a row of boards nailed together. No roof.

Rosemary pulls off the road and parks beside the only cinder-block building in the whole camp. For all its flaking paint and rusted tin roof, it stands like a solid fortress among crumbling ruins. "This is the camp store," she says, which I'd already figured out.

She points to another building a few hundred yards away by the edge of a wooded area. "Over there, that's where the outhouses are."

I don't need to look. I can smell them from where we sit.

Rosemary climbs out of the pickup. "I'm not taking your daddy's truck the rest of the way," she says. "It might scare some folks."

I want to ask her how my dad's truck could scare anybody, but I don't. I'm afraid she will tell me his truck has been here before. Has maybe even carried men with torches who set people's clothes on fire.

I follow Rosemary. We walk close to the row buildings. I am eye-level with the windows, looking into rooms that are lit by a single naked lightbulb hanging from the ceiling. I see only some beds lining the walls and a few orange crates. Used as what? Chairs? Tables? Some have clothes piled in them.

The whole way here I have been wondering why Rosemary has brought me along. She could just as easily have gotten word to Gator and the others on her own, which was why

I came to her in the first place. But now I realize she wants me to see all this for myself. She wants me to understand what it's like, living in this camp. Travis Waite's camp.

"Up ahead . . . that's what they call the bunkhouse," Rosemary says. "The unmarried men rent space there." She slows her steps and looks over at me. "My daddy would skin me within an inch of my life if he knew I was over here."

So would mine, I'm thinking, even though my dad has never laid a hand on me.

We walk toward the bunkhouse at the end of the dirt road. Somebody has a radio on. Jerry Lee Lewis is pounding out "Great Balls of Fire" on the piano keys. We pass a rusted Buick parked between two shacks, which seems to have been converted into somebody's bedroom. The tires are gone. The car sits up on cinder blocks. Somebody's feet are sticking out the back window.

Voices, low and anxious, drift back to us from a group of men on the porch of the bunkhouse. Rosemary pulls me over to the side of the building and lifts a finger to her lips. "Stay here," she whispers, then disappears around the front.

A few minutes later Rosemary's head appears around the corner. In the dark, it looks as if it's floating above the ground, bodiless. She signals me to come with her. When I round the corner, the men look up. I count seven of them. There is a light on inside the building, which is nothing but a big open room with rows and rows of bunk beds. The only light on the porch comes from a kerosene lantern.

"I told them you're here with me," she says.

Well, of course she did. I understand that now. I am the daughter of the enemy. I am not to be trusted.

For the first time since we drove up to this place, I am scared. I am in a migrant camp for colored folks—a white girl, standing here in front of a bunch of Negro men who are sitting on an open porch late at night staring at me. Every terrifying, ugly story I have ever heard about colored men doing unspeakable things to white girls comes crashing down on me, and the weight of those stories almost brings me to my knees.

Chuck Berry is belting out "Johnny B. Goode" from a black-and-white transistor radio that leans against Gator's hip. *Gator.* I feel the air returning to my lungs.

Seven dark faces are watching me. Their eyes shine like coal in the flickering light of the lantern. I recognize the two men I overheard that day in our groves, the mustache man and the barrel man. Gator looks down at me. He doesn't bother to stand. None of them do. "Rosemary says you got something to tell us."

I can't seem to find the words I need. I stand here, at the bottom of the steps, dumb as a fence post. Somewhere in my mind I have made important connections. I know tonight's Klan meeting has something to do with this small group of men. I don't know how I know this, I just do. The problem is, I don't know how to put it in words that will make any sense to them. Words that will convince them they are in danger.

"I thought you should know the Klan's up to something." I finally manage to get this much out.

Gator and three of the men laugh. Then he turns to the others and says something in Spanish. The other three men laugh.

Gator turns back to me. "When *isn't* the Klan up to something?"

"I think it has to do with you and the other pickers," I tell him.

"Why would you think that?"

I look over at Rosemary. She's being no help at all. Like the rest of them, she's waiting for my answer. She sits down on the top step.

I don't dare tell them where I've been tonight or why. I haven't even told Rosemary this. "There's been rumors going around town," I tell them. "Some folks are saying the pickers are setting all these fires."

"Why would we do that?" Rosemary says. I don't miss the *we*.

"I'm not saying you did. It's what the people in town think. They think you've got it in for somebody."

One of the men says something in Spanish to some of the others. They're all staring at me. The man says, "*Su padre*, he is in the Klan? Is this how you know these things?"

Gator is staring hard at my face. I look away.

Rosemary says, "Dove's just trying to help is all. She wanted to warn you there's trouble coming."

"We ain't done nothin'," one of the men says. I notice he isn't wearing a shirt. His skin is slick with sweat. A large red welt runs from his shoulder across his chest. Blood is crusted in spots. I have seen this plenty of times before. The strap from his picking bag has cut through his skin. Pickers in our groves sometimes have to stop work early because of bleeding sores.

"I'm not saying you did," I tell him. "I think the Klan's using whatever they can as an excuse. It doesn't make any sense, I know, but . . ."

Rosemary goes over to Gator and sits next to him. "I told her about Travis bringing in Julio and the others. Taking their wages to pay for him driving them here."

"I know Travis has been keeping some of you in debt, overcharging you," I say, "taking your pay to cover bills at the store and your rent before you ever see the money."

Gator looks up at me. "You think we've been setting fires to get back at Travis Waite?"

"No. But a lot of folks in these parts know Travis owns this camp. And that's what *they're* thinking."

"We never set no fires," one of the men says. He's not much older than Gator. He's missing part of one earlobe and several teeth. "No point in that."

A baby begins to cry. Its sharp, piercing shrieks cut through the night. The barrel man gets to his feet and heads back toward the long row building. I watch him disappear through one of the doors.

"That's Julio Gonzalez," Rosemary says. "His son is only a few weeks old. He's one of the men who's in debt to Travis."

"There has to be some reason you've got the Klan nervous." I look at Gator when I say this.

He doesn't answer.

Rosemary looks over at him. He glances from her to me.

"It's nothing more than talk right now," Gator says.

"What kind of talk?"

"We're thinking maybe if we stick together, maybe not show up for work for a few days, they'll figure it out."

"Figure what out?"

"They need us. If we don't work, the fruit'll rot on the trees. The tomatoes, the strawberries, the pole beans, they'll all rot."

"Are you saying you're going on strike? Like union folks?"

"Maybe." Gator takes a deep breath. "Someday. Not right now. We're not organized enough. It's like I told you. It's just talk."

"But Travis must know you've been talking about it," I say.

Gator shrugs. He turns the radio up louder.

I look over at Rosemary. "Let's go," I tell her.

No one says anything as we walk away. But I can feel six pairs of coal black eyes searing themselves right into my back.

Five minutes later Rosemary climbs out of the driver's seat in front of Luellen's place. I scoot over behind the wheel. "You going to be okay driving home?" she says.

"I got myself here, didn't I?" What she doesn't know is that I'm not planning to go home. Not right away. I've got one more thing I need to do tonight before I can lay my head on my pillow.

20

The gravel I've scooped up from the driveway hits Chase's half-open window and the side of the house like a barrage of bullets.

It's after midnight. His T-bird is parked out back of the house. I checked. I fire off another round of stones. And wait.

I'm getting ready to fling another fistful when a voice from behind me says, "Whoa! Hold your fire."

I about fly out of my skin. My heart shifts into full throttle. It's racing like a motorboat engine at top speed. Chase puts his hands on my shoulders and tries to calm me down. "Hey, Dove, it's okay."

I pull away and take a step back.

"You jerk! Creep! Don't you dare touch me."

He frowns and looks up at his window. "I thought this was a friendly call."

"You're an idiot!"

"Okay! I get the general idea. What're you doing here, then? You come here in the middle of the night just to call me names? Is that it?" He gives me the once-over and shakes his head. "Where you been? You're a mess."

"And you're a liar!" I yell. "And . . ." My voice begins to break. "You're in the Klan." The last word comes out as a sob. I turn away.

"I'm not in the Klan," he says.

"I saw you."

"Saw me? Where?"

I tell him about following my dad. Suddenly it dawns on me that my dad is probably home by now too. Maybe he's got the police out looking for whoever it was stole his pickup. Maybe he'll think whoever stole it took me along too. Kidnapped me. Maybe I will just let him go on thinking that. Maybe I'll get back in this truck and keep on going till I reach California.

I head to the pickup.

Chase runs alongside me. "Are you listening? I'm *not* in the Klan."

"You were there."

"My dad dragged me along. He makes me come with him sometimes."

"You don't have to go. You could tell him no."

"Come on, Dove. You know how he is."

This is true. I do know. Jacob Tully could scare the bark off a tree when he's feeling mean.

"So it's just easier this way, going along with it?" I ask.

"Well, yeah. Better than getting the crap beat out of me."

"I hate that you're part of this. I hate you for it."

"Dove, I'm *not* part of it."

He has his hand on my arm. I am trying to climb into the driver's seat. "Yes, you *are*." Chase lets go of my arm. "What did they talk about, then? You say you're not a part of it, then you can tell me. They're planning something, aren't they?"

Chase puts his hand over mine, the one clutching the steering wheel. His touch is hot and damp. "Yeah. They're planning something."

"What?" I slide my hand from under his.

"I can't tell you that."

"Why not?"

"Because I can't, Dove. You're just going to have to trust me on this."

But I don't listen. I don't believe him for a minute. I know what I saw at Spudder's. I turn the key in the ignition and drown out his stupid excuses. He jumps out of the way as I back up the truck, whip it around, and tear down the driveway, the tires spitting stones every inch of the way.

* * * * * * * * * * * * * * * * *

Right now I'm the walking dead. I am so tired from all that's been going on tonight, I'm about ready to keel over. But I can't do that because my dad is sitting in the rocker on the back porch, waiting for me when I drive up. I muster all the energy I have left. I'm going to need it.

I stand at the foot of the steps. Dad stays in the rocker. The same one I sat in the night Chase told me about Gus.

"Where you been?" he asks.

"Driving."

"Driving where?"

"Around."

"With just a permit?"

I don't bother to tell him I left my permit at home. "I'm getting my license in less than four weeks. It's not like I don't know how to drive, Dad."

"You take off with my pickup without telling me. You don't leave a note. What am I supposed to think?"

"You do it all the time," I tell him. "You take off, don't tell me where you're going. Most of the time I don't know where the heck you are."

Dad is on his feet now. We square off and size each other up like two cowboys facing each other down in the middle of a dusty street, their fingers twitching only inches from their guns.

Dad is the first to look away. He draws a deep breath. "You had me worried." His voice is low, almost a whisper.

"Well, I'm home. I'm in one piece. No dents in the pickup, if that's what you're worried about." The sharp anger in my voice rings in my ears. There's no hiding it.

"I swear, if you weren't going to be sixteen in a few weeks, I'd whale the daylights out of you for going off like that." He rubs his eyes with his thumb and forefinger, like he's trying to squeeze that picture out of his head. "Look at yourself!"

I stare down at my filthy clothes, at the scratches and dirt on my arms and legs, at a few sandspurs Rosemary missed. There isn't a whole lot I can say.

"Get on up to your room," Dad growls. He jerks his thumb toward the house.

I head through the door, hoping this is the end of it. But Dad grabs my arm as I'm passing by. "This isn't over by a long shot, Dove."

"What's not over?"

"This. You behaving like this." He follows me into the kitchen. "Coming home late for dinner. Staying out all hours. Taking my pickup without permission. Where in tarnation is this coming from?"

"Maybe I get it from you," I say.

His face turns the color of raspberry sherbet. It looks blotchy in the glare of the overhead fluorescent light. He stares into my face like I'm some complete stranger who has just walked into his kitchen. I know how he feels.

I leave him standing there and head down the hall.

I am lying on my bed, staring up at the ceiling, thinking about Chase and how it felt, seeing him at that meeting tonight, when Dad shows up at my bedroom door.

"You think you can just take off like that, in my pickup, anytime you feel like it and not get punished?"

I don't answer him. He's not there. As far as I'm concerned, my dad—the one I thought I knew—is gone. Forever. I keep my eyes on the ceiling.

"From now on I want you home right after school, you hear? Every day for the next two weeks." Even with my eyes on the ceiling, I know he's poking the air with his finger a few times for emphasis. "And I want you home on the weekends. No parties or movies."

I swing my legs over the side of the bed and sit up. I have

been giving a lot of thought to what I'm going to say next. Now I'm wondering if I have the courage to do it. I turn to Dad and look him right in the eye.

"I want to tell Delia about Travis," I say.

He blinks a few times, looking confused. "What about Travis?"

"About him killing Gus Washburn."

Dad stands there like somebody facing a firing squad. "Where'd you hear that?" He crams his hands into his pockets.

"Doesn't matter where or how. I just know is all."

Dad takes a step forward. His pockets are bulging with his fists. "You aren't gonna do anything but cause pain by telling Delia. What happened to Gus happened a long time ago. It was an accident. Nobody's to blame."

"How can you say that, Dad? Gus is dead. He's dead because Travis Waite was having what he likes to call a little fun. Everybody in town knows Gus was killed in a hit-and-run. They just don't know who was driving that car. But Cholly Blue saw the whole thing. Delia told me. And Cholly says the driver aimed that car right at Gus, like it was some kind of loaded weapon or something. On *purpose,* Dad."

"You don't know anything about it, Dove. You try to stir up trouble now, the only one's gonna get hurt is Delia." Dad shakes his head, looking solemn. His voice is quiet and even, but I know all that calm is hiding a powerful lot of anger. It's like lava boiling down under the earth, waiting for the right moment to explode. I can feel it.

"How can you look Delia in the eye every day, knowing what you do?" I ask.

Dad lowers his head, exposing the top of his crew cut.

The hair is thin enough on top that I catch a glimpse of sun-burned scalp. When he looks up, I can tell he's struggling to make his face look normal.

When he has control of himself, he says, "I thought I was doing the right thing for Delia. Seemed to me with Gus gone and her boy Jeremiah heading off to college, she needed to go on working; she needed things to stay like they'd always been. I couldn't bring Gus back, but I could make sure Delia's life didn't change any more than it already had. And I could watch over her, make sure she was taken care of. I owed Gus that."

"Dad, what we owe Gus, *and* Delia, is justice."

He shakes his head. "This case won't ever come to trial, Dove. You've lived in this town long enough to know that."

"There are folks higher up, with more power than Spud-der Rhodes or the county sheriff, folks who can make sure Gus gets justice."

Dad shrugs. "Maybe," he concedes. "But with the only eyewitness being Cholly, and Spudder and them sticking to-gether on Travis's and Jimmy's stories—"

"Chase knows the truth," I say. "He overheard Travis telling Jacob what happened." I feel bad about breaking my word to Chase. Never in my life have I sworn to keep a secret and then told. But I'm not feeling too kindly toward him right now, not after seeing him at that meeting.

Dad tips his head back and squints up at the overhead light. He sighs. "Chase won't go against his father."

"If Chase won't testify, maybe you could." I say this softly, more to myself than Dad.

Dad is looking at me as if I've completely lost my marbles.

"Well, Travis talked to you about it, didn't he? Or Jacob told you. Somebody did. If you testified—"

Dad's fists are bulging in his pockets again. "When are you gonna understand, Dove? I've got to live in this town. Things have been getting bad around here of late. There's a lot of folks upset about these fires. If you tell Delia about Travis, if she goes to the police and tries to stir up trouble—" He pulls his hands from his pockets and braces himself on the doorjamb. "Look, I grew up with Travis and Spudder and Jimmy and them. I'm not about to turn on them. Not even for Delia."

I cross the room. I'm standing only a few feet from Dad. "Then I don't want to live here anymore. Not in this house. Not with you."

He narrows his eyes at me. "And where do you think you're going to go?"

"It doesn't matter. Anywhere. Even that disgusting migrant camp would be better than living with a member of the Klan."

When the slap catches the side of my face, it's as if somebody hit me with a gunstock. Never in all my born days has my dad ever laid a hand on me, even though he has threatened to.

The tears make it hard for me to see his face. It's like trying to see him under water. I tell myself this man, standing across from me, isn't my father, *can't* be my father. This man isn't the same person I've been living with all these years, who has made sure I had everything I needed, who I thought loved me.

Dad stretches his hand toward me. I jump back. His arm

flops to his side like a tree limb half severed in a storm. That's when I see his eyes are wet too. "Dove," he says, and shakes his head, "listen to me, I'm—"

"Get out of my room!" I scream. "Get *out*!" I can't bear to look at his face. But he saves me the trouble by turning around and softly closing the door behind him.

A few hours later I show up at Delia's door in the gray dawn. I have walked the whole two miles to town, carrying one of Dad's old duffel bags packed with a few changes of clothes, a toothbrush, and my school books. My arms feel like they're about to snap off.

Delia's house is in the colored quarters. I have never been here before, not in all the years she has worked for us, although I know the address. White folks don't go to the colored quarters unless they have business to attend to, which isn't very often.

The colored section is surrounded on two sides by railroad tracks, the Seaboard to the south and the Atlantic Coastline to the east. Delia's house is on a dirt road. None of the streets in the colored quarters are paved. Her house is a small one-story, not much bigger than Luellen's apartment but with a front porch and window boxes bursting with petunias.

Delia stands in the doorway in a worn terry-cloth robe covered with swirling blue and pink flowers that could make you dizzy if you looked at them too long. I stare at the robe. I can't help thinking of the one Delia was wearing the night Gus died, the one that had Gus's blood all over it. On her head is what looks to be part of an old nylon stocking that has been cut off near the top and tied in a little knot. She blinks a few times, as if she is waking from a dream.

She sticks her head out the door and looks up and down the road. "You walk here all the way yourself, child?"

I look down at my feet. "I got something I need to tell you," I say.

She swings the screen door open for me. "Well, come on in then." She points to the couch in the cramped living room, then heads off somewhere.

Against the far wall, boards have been stacked on cinder blocks to make bookshelves. Almost every shelf is full. The rest of the wall space is taken up with photographs. Dozens and dozens of photographs stuck on with tape or thumbtacks. I recognize Gus and Jeremiah. The others, I suspect, are Delia's older children and her grandchildren.

The smell of fresh coffee perking fills the tiny room.

Delia comes back a few minutes later, carrying a tray with two cups of coffee, sugar, cream, and a plate of biscuits. She scoops two heaping spoonfuls of sugar into my coffee and goes heavy on the cream. She knows this is how I like it.

I sit in an old rocker made from tree branches with the bark still on them and take the cup from her. While Delia stirs a little sweetness into her coffee, I look over at the books again.

"They're from Jeremiah," she tells me. "When he's finished with a course, he sends the books to me. He says they belong to me because I paid for them. I figure if I read 'em all, I'll practically have myself a college education. Now he's gone on to graduate school, even thinking about getting himself a Ph.D. Isn't that something? Dr. Jeremiah Washburn." She shakes her head. "Never in all my born days did I ever dream . . ." Delia's voice drifts off. She's eyeing my duffel.

"What you got in that bag?"

"A few things."

"You running away again?"

When I was little, I was always running away from home for one reason or another. Usually Delia would pack me a few jelly sandwiches, and I'd be back in time for dinner. But I haven't done that in years.

"Delia," I say, "I've got some upsetting news. Real upsetting. But if I tell you, I'm scared that things are going to change."

"Change how?"

I shake my head and look away. I don't have an answer for this.

"If you got something to say, it's up to you whether you say it or not."

When I don't speak right up, Delia moves forward and sits rigid on the edge of the couch. She is wearing huge fluffy slippers that make it look as if two pink Persian cats are wrapped around her feet. She clamps her hands on her knees. *"How's* it gonna change my life?"

"I don't know," I say. "Things are going to change, but how they change . . . I guess that'll be up to you."

She narrows her eyes at me. "This is about Gus, isn't it?"

My hands are shaking. Some of the coffee spills into the saucer.

"You tell me the truth, girl." Delia's eyes burn right through me. "I've been waiting six years for it. I got a right to it. Even if it means my whole world comes crashing down in flames."

My mouth is so dry I'm not sure I can even get the first word out. Trickles of sweat run along the sides of my face. I try to take a sip of coffee, but it comes right back up and dribbles down my chin. I wipe it away with my hand and set my cup back on the tray.

Delia is waiting. She doesn't say a word.

It takes me a while to get into the story, but the more I talk the faster my mouth goes, words just tumble out, about Chase telling me about Jimmy Wheeler and Travis Waite, and about me telling my dad last night. But I don't say anything about them being in the Klan.

This whole time Delia's expression never changes. Her hands are folded in her lap, like she is praying her way through all this, praying that what she's hearing is all some terrible mistake.

When I'm done talking, we both sit there. It's my turn to wait. The silence in the room is deafening in that way a heavy rain can be, blocking out everything so it feels like the rumbling is coming from inside your head.

After a few minutes Delia says, "All those years that white trash Travis Waite coming to the back door, wanting me to fetch him this, fetch him that, smiling that ugly sneer of his. All that time, knowing he'd killed my Gus, and never once looking sorry about it."

Delia's eyes are wet, but I know she won't let herself cry in front of me. "And your *daddy,* him *knowing* it, and never letting on, just expecting me to go on cooking his meals, washing his dirty underwear, cleaning his house, like it didn't matter one bit that his crew boss killed my man." She chokes out these last few words and covers her mouth with her hand.

Delia closes her eyes. She crosses her arms over her chest and rocks herself back and forth. Rocking. Rocking. When she finally stops, she opens her eyes and the look in them is a terrible sight. I stare down at my hands, lying there like two dead white fish in my lap.

"I thought your daddy was different." She shakes her head. "All this time, there I was, thinking he cared about me." Delia looks over at me, and it's all I can do not to burst out crying myself. My whole body starts to shake from holding in those tears.

"He does care, Delia. I know he does. He just doesn't always do the right thing."

Delia's on her feet, carrying the tray back to the kitchen. "You better run along now," she says. The sound of her slippered feet, scuffing along the worn floorboards, drifts farther away. I follow her down the hall to the kitchen. Sunlight pours through the window over the small porcelain sink and across the checkered oilcloth on the table. It slides down the walls like melted butter, making everything shimmer. It is so bright it hurts my eyes.

"Delia, let me help."

She slams the tray on the table so hard one of the cups topples over, spilling coffee. "Help! How you gonna help?" She throws a dishtowel at the tray. Within seconds it's a soggy brown.

"You best be getting on home."

"Delia—"

"And you can tell your daddy I won't be coming to make his breakfast this morning." She looks up from the mess on the table. "You tell him I don't think I'll bother making him breakfast ever again."

The whole time I was walking here, preparing myself to tell her the truth, I knew this is how it would turn out. Knew Delia would quit working for us. Knew she would walk out of our lives as if she'd never been a part of them. I knew it, but I still hoped it wouldn't happen.

"Maybe you could get a lawyer," I tell her.

She laughs so hard she starts to cry. "Go home," she says. "Go on, get out of here." She is close to yelling at me. I back out of the kitchen.

I stop in the living room to get my duffel bag. For some reason I had it in my head when I left the house this morning that maybe I could stay with Delia for a few days, until I could figure out what to do. I can see now I wasn't thinking straight. The last person Delia wants hanging around her house is the person who just brought her whole world crashing down in flames.

Outside, the petunias—red, yellow, dark violet, lavender,

white, pink, fuchsia—cascade over the window boxes like rainbow waterfalls in the bright morning sun. I stare at them as all sorts of thoughts rip through my head: *Did I do the right thing, telling Delia the truth? Did I do it for the right reason? For Delia? Or did I do it to ease my own conscience? Did I tell her what I did to get back at Travis? Did I do it because I am mad as hell at Dad?* Which would have definitely been the wrong reason. Now I'm wondering if maybe my dad was right. Maybe it would have been better to let things be. Telling Delia the truth isn't going to bring Gus back.

I want to believe I came here because we owed it to Delia to tell her what happened. Only now she has no job. No way to pay for a lawyer so she can get some sort of justice. And I don't have her in my life anymore. I can't help thinking this is an awful price to pay for the truth.

All the colors of the petunias have started to run together in one watery blur. I don't even make it to the end of her street before the flood of tears knocks me to my knees. Delia's isn't the only world that is crashing down in flames. I slip behind a hedge of honeysuckle, pull myself into a tight ball, and bury my face in my arms.

* * * * * * * * * * * * * * *

It is ten blocks to Luellen Sutter's place. By the time I get there, the sun is on full blast, baking everything in sight.

The first thing that catches my eye is a big collage of cardboard taped over the place where Luellen's shop window used to be. Tiny pieces of shattered glass, tucked in the groove where the sidewalk meets the brick wall, gleam like a row of diamonds. The big pieces have been swept up.

Luellen stands in the doorway of her apartment in her uniform, holding her white shoes in one hand. She doesn't bat an eyelash. I suspect she's getting used to me showing up unannounced.

Rosemary comes walking down the little hallway from the bathroom. She's wearing baby-doll pajamas and her hair is still in rollers. She takes in my face, which I know is all puffy and red, and then the duffel bag. "You going somewheres?" she asks.

"Don't know yet." This is the truth. I have no idea where I am going next. I'm not even sure why I came here.

"What happened to your window?" I ask Luellen. I drop my duffel and sit on the edge of the unmade sofa bed without being invited.

"Hooligans." She pours a cup of coffee and sets it next to me on the end table. "Sorry I can't hang around and visit with y'all, but Saturday's my busiest day. Got to get the shop set up." She sticks her feet—first one then the other—up on the chair and ties her shoelaces. "And I got me a little extra cleaning up to do this morning." She turns to Rosemary and gives her a look. "You be downstairs by eight-thirty now, you hear?" she says as she grabs the doorknob.

We listen to Luellen's footsteps descending the stairs.

"Hooligans?" I say to Rosemary.

"They threw a few rocks through the shop window last night."

"Any messages come with those rocks?" I ask.

Rosemary pulls something out of the trash and hands it to

me: a rock the size of a softball with NIGGER LOVER printed in red paint.

She sits beside me on the sofa bed. I notice little dabs of Clearasil on her face.

"Why Luellen's place?"

"Why do you think?"

I figure this probably has something to do with her and Gator being friends.

"But who—"

Rosemary begins taking the rollers out of her hair and stacking them in a little pile. "I don't know, but I got a few ideas."

So do I. This rock has Willy Podd's name written all over it.

She combs her fingers through her hair, loosening the curls. "What are you doing here, anyway?"

This time I don't hold back. I tell her everything that's happened, including the part about Chase and my dad being at the Klan meeting. By the time I'm finished, I'm like a balloon that's had all the air let out of it. I just want to crawl off somewhere and sleep for a year.

Rosemary gets up and drifts around the kitchen, making toast that neither of us eats. She pours me a cup of coffee, even though I haven't touched the one Luellen gave me. She shuffles through boxes of cereal in the cabinet above the sink.

Finally I say, "Sit down, Rosemary. You're making me nervous."

Rosemary does what I ask. She slumps in a kitchen chair and folds her arms across her chest. "I trusted you," she says. "I took you to the camp."

"So I could warn the pickers something was going to happen," I remind her.

She leans toward me, arms still folded. "Your daddy and your boyfriend are in the Klan, Dove. The *Klan,* for heaven's sake."

"Rosemary, what the Klan is doing is wrong. Dad and Chase are wrong. I'm not going to betray you or any of the pickers. I will swear to that on the Bible. I'm trying to help is all."

She chews on her lower lip, giving what I've said some thought. "Did you know Eli's sick?" she says. "He wasn't in the groves yesterday, and Travis—" She stops. Her eyes dart from one corner of the room to another, like she's afraid Travis Waite might suddenly pop out of the woodwork.

"What about Travis?" Just the mention of his name sours my stomach.

"He's going to think Eli is doing it on purpose. He'll make things bad for him."

"But if Eli's sick, why would— What's wrong with him, anyway? Eli, I mean."

"Nobody's sure. He looked poorly the day before yesterday. Had the chills and all. Most everybody thinks he's got the fever. But a few of the pickers, they're thinking it might be the new pesticide they've been using. Some of them have been getting headaches and sore throats. Eli, he's old. You know? Maybe it's worse for him."

"Has he seen a doctor?"

Rosemary stares at me and frowns. "The pickers don't have money for doctors."

"Eli's not a picker," I remind her. "I mean, he helps with

the picking, sometimes. But he's not seasonal. He works most of the year in our groves."

"Oh, well, then of course he can afford a doctor. He must be rolling in money."

Rosemary's comeback is like Dad's slap all over again. "Do you know where Eli lives?" I ask.

"Yes."

"Can you take me there?"

"Well, not right now. I gotta go to work, remember?" She stands and points to the unmade sofa bed. "You look about dead on your feet anyway. You should get some sleep."

I collapse onto the sofa bed and drift into unconsciousness for the next nine hours. When Rosemary wakes me, it is past five. She has changed into faded plaid Bermuda shorts and a blue sleeveless blouse.

I doze in Rosemary's rusted green Ford that she's named the Green Hornet while she drives us to Eli's place, even though the noise from the hole in her tailpipe is loud enough to wake the dead.

Rosemary having her own car came as a complete surprise. Not that it's much of a car. It's probably close to twenty years old. When I asked her where she got it, she said that it had been sitting out back of the camp and didn't belong to anybody. Gator and one of the other pickers found parts in the junkyard and got it up and running for her.

Rosemary pulls up in front of Eli's place. There is no garage or driveway. A single lemon tree stands in the front yard.

Eli's house is a tiny white cinder-block building in a little cluster of similar buildings, some painted blue, others green.

The road is dirt with no curb, like the colored quarters in Benevolence. The houses are just off the main highway, across from a Texaco station and a Winn-Dixie. The place isn't all that far from the turnoff to the migrant camp—maybe a few hundred yards.

No one answers our knock. The door is unlocked. Rosemary pokes her head inside and calls Eli's name.

We step into the semidark living room. The shades are drawn. The floors are covered in worn linoleum that is supposed to resemble wood but isn't even close. There are only a few sticks of furniture—a lumpy-looking sofa and one overstuffed chair with tape x'ed over a large tear on the arm, but the place is real tidy. Faded plastic roses are parked in a vase on the kitchen table.

Photographs are taped to the wall, which makes me think of Delia. I swallow back my tears as Rosemary knocks on a door across the narrow hall from the kitchen. Inside we find Eli, tangled in gray sheets and still in his work clothes, except for his boots, which lie on the floor by his bed.

His lips are crusted white; his eyes are glassy. I can't be sure he even sees us. I put my hand on his forehead. He is burning up.

I grab Rosemary's arm. "We have to get him to a hospital." I can tell by the expression on her face that she had no idea Eli was this sick.

She loosens my grip and signals me to follow her back into the kitchen. "I don't think we should try to move him, Dove."

"We can find a doctor, maybe get him to come here."

"You know a doctor who treats black folks?"

"Some around here do. They got separate entrances into their office. One for whites, one for coloreds."

"Yeah, but will they come all the way out here to treat a black man who isn't going to be able to pay them one red cent?" The whole time Rosemary is talking, she's rummaging through the kitchen cabinets until she finds a glass. She works the pump at the sink until the stream of rusty water begins to look reasonably clear. She fills the glass and hands it to me. "Try to get him to drink some of this," she says.

I hold Eli's head up and put the glass to his lips. His eyes roll back in his head. He lets out a soft groan.

Rosemary comes in with a pot filled with cool water. She sits on the edge of the bed and unbuttons Eli's shirt partway. Then she dips a threadbare hand towel in the pot, wrings it out, and sponges Eli's face and chest. All the while she whispers comforting words, telling him things are going to be all right.

I smooth out the tangled sheets and tuck them in. I take Eli's coarse old hand in mine and tell him that we are going to take care of him.

Sweat is pouring off all three of us. It's like an oven in this house.

"You think he's got a fan?" I ask Rosemary.

She shrugs. We look in all the closets and cabinets until we find a small fan. It scrapes and clatters when we turn it on and put it by the only window in the bedroom. But at least now the air is moving.

"How come no one's here looking after him? Where are his boys?" I know for a fact that Eli raised four sons on his own after his wife died.

"Gone up north," Rosemary says. "Gator told me they went looking for factory work in Ohio and Michigan years ago. They probably don't even know Eli's sick."

I leave Rosemary with Eli and wander through his house, which doesn't take long. Living room, kitchen, bedroom, no bathroom—just an outhouse—and one other tiny bedroom, with only a single bed and a wooden crate for a nightstand. The bed is nothing more than an old stained box spring and mattress on the floor. No sheets or blankets.

All that I find in the cabinet are half a box of Rice Krispies cereal, a can of tomato soup, and some stale saltines. The milk in the refrigerator smells sour. I dump it into the sink. It is the only thing I can think to do. If Delia were here, she'd know what to do. She'd take good care of Eli.

I try not to think about what my life is going to be like without Delia in it, but the tears come anyway. I stand there holding the empty milk carton, swatting the tears away with my free hand. I'm scared to death for Eli. And I don't know who to turn to for help.

I toss the milk carton in the trash and close the cabinet doors. We need food. Delia has always done the grocery shopping for Dad and me. But I figure this is one thing I can do on my own. I dig through my purse, pull out my wallet, and count out three dollars and seventy-two cents. All the money I have in the world. I pull a scrap of paper from my purse and scribble down a few items.

Rosemary is trying to get Eli to drink more water when I come back to the bedroom. It dribbles down his chin, soaking his chest and shirt.

"I'm going over to the Winn-Dixie for groceries," I tell

her. "When I get back, could you go get my duffel bag? I left it at Luellen's."

"You thinking of staying here?"

"Eli needs somebody to look after him and I need a place to stay," I say. "You got any better ideas?"

The sun is setting by the time Rosemary gets back. She sets my duffel on the couch and plunks down an old beat-up brown suitcase next to it.

"What's that?"

"*My* things."

"Rosemary, I can take care of Eli by myself. You don't have to do this." The truth is, I've been worried sick about how I was going to nurse Eli on my own. I'm so grateful for Rosemary's help, I could cry.

"It's either stay here and help you or find space even a sardine couldn't fit into in my folks' trailer." She takes stock of the situation, going from room to room, like I did earlier. "I'll sleep on the couch. You can have that other bedroom."

"What happened? What about your job?"

Rosemary goes to the kitchen and looks through the grocery bag on the counter to see what I bought at Winn-Dixie. "You forgot coffee."

"I got instant."

She makes a face. Then she lowers herself onto one of the kitchen chairs. A sorry wad of stuffing peeks out of a split in the plastic seat cover. "Luellen said it would be better if I went back to live with my folks, seeing as how there's people sending me messages by way of her shop window in the middle of the night. She says I'll be safer with Ma and Daddy. What she means is *she'll* be safer with me not there. And her customers won't be scared off."

"I'm real sorry."

"Yeah. Me too."

We spend the next half hour heating Campbell's chicken noodle soup and taking turns trying to get some nourishment into Eli. He doesn't seem to know who we are, and that's got us worried.

While Eli kneads the sheets with his fingers in a restless sleep, we make some peanut butter and jelly sandwiches and sit down on the lumpy sofa. The cockroaches in this place know no fear. They creep along the baseboards, scoot across the kitchen floor, up and down the cabinets, and across the counter, even though the lights are still on. We have given up pounding them with our sneakers.

Rosemary gets up to shift the rabbit ears on Eli's old TV.

She tries them every which way she can. But all we can get is one fuzzy station out of Miami.

Being with Rosemary isn't anything like being with Rayanne or Jinny. We don't talk about boys—well, Gator's name has come up a few times, but I've never told her much about Chase and me. We don't talk about clothes or music or who's going out with who and what they're doing. It's different. Even though she's only a grade ahead of me, Rosemary seems a lot older sometimes. It's a little like having a big sister. But other times, like the afternoon we skipped school, she seems kind of fragile, younger. I just don't know what to make of her.

I brush the sandwich crumbs from my blouse. "We got ourselves a problem," I tell her while she's working those rabbit ears.

She looks over her shoulder at me and raises her eyebrows. "I think we got us a whole shit pot full of problems."

I about choke on my sandwich when Rosemary says this. I've never heard her use words like that before. We look at each other and suddenly we both burst out laughing. It doesn't make a lick of sense, but we can't seem to stop. I'm laughing so hard my side aches.

Rosemary flops down on the couch next to me.

"Okay, I'm being serious now," I tell her. "All I have left is ninety-three cents."

"I've got a little money. It'll be okay."

"But we can't stay here forever."

"I'm not planning to. As soon as Eli's better, I'm gonna look for another job. If I have to, I'll go back to picking."

"What about school?"

She shrugs and gets up to give the rabbit ears another try. I get the feeling there have been plenty of times in Rosemary's life when she didn't go to school because she had to help her family out with the picking.

At least Rosemary has a plan. Every time I let myself think beyond the next minute, I stop breathing. It's like having an elephant sitting on my chest.

You don't sleep very well when you don't know if tomorrow you'll have a roof over your head or enough money to buy so much as a loaf of bread. This is why I am still wide awake at two in the morning when a rumble of car horns suddenly thunders down the highway and onto the dirt road by Eli's house.

At first I don't think much about the noise. Just some folks coming back from a wild Saturday night at a juke joint, probably. When the racket doesn't let up any, I stumble out into the living room. Lights from outside are flickering through gashes torn in the shade.

Rosemary is hunkered down below the windowsill. She waves her hand, signaling for me to get down. I crawl across the floor.

"What's going on?"

Rosemary is shaking so bad, she can hardly talk. "I don't know," she whispers.

I lift the corner of the shade and peek out. A whole caravan of trucks and cars is weaving through this little colored village, blowing horns and flashing high beams.

The pickups and cars creep down the dirt road two by two, so nobody can pass them. Anybody coming from the other direction would have to either pull up onto somebody's front yard—there being no driveways— or back up, because there is no getting by these folks.

The horns are so loud, I put my hands over my ears.

When the silence finally comes, it's like being under water. I can feel the pressure building.

A voice thunders through the night. "Get out here, you worthless old nigger." The voice belongs to Travis Waite. Rosemary and I exchange panicky looks. We both know it's the Klan out there. And all I can think is that my dad and Chase must be with them. I've been gone since before dawn, although my dad probably doesn't know I left that early. What he does know for certain is that I didn't come home tonight.

"What do they want with Eli?" I ask.

Rosemary has started to cry. "They probably think he's part of the slowdown, him missing work and all."

"The what?"

"The slowdown. It's what I started to tell you this morning, about Travis maybe coming after Eli."

"That's what Gator meant last night when he was talking about the pickers not showing up for work for a few days, isn't it? I thought he said it was just talk. They weren't really doing anything yet."

Rosemary shakes her head and wipes the tears from her face. She puts her hand on my shoulder. Her hand is soaking wet and clammy. "It's been going on for a few weeks now."

"What? But—"

She shakes her head and waves her hand at me. "Not now, Dove."

I lift the corner of the shade again.

The trucks and cars behind the two lead pickups have all

turned their headlights toward Eli's house. Some of the men are standing outside their cars, hanging around talking and smoking. It's hard to tell if any of them have been drinking. If they are liquored up, things could get real ugly. Nobody is wearing white robes or hoods. They are dressed in their everyday clothes, like normal folks. Only there isn't anything *normal* about what they are doing here.

A cockroach skitters across my bare foot, but I don't let go of the shade.

Travis Waite stands in front of his pickup. He is nothing more than a dark silhouette. But I know it's him. I see the skunk tail hanging from his antenna. He sends a stream of tobacco juice right onto the base of Eli's lemon tree.

It's hard to pick out the other faces with all those bright headlights shining in my eyes, which I guess is the point. Headlights. White hoods. Same thing. Klan folks manage to scare people half to death and hide their identity while they're doing it.

But in spite of those glaring headlights I can still pick out Willy Podd, hanging around the back of Macon Podd's pickup. Macon Podd is Willy's dad. There's no sign of Earl, though, which surprises me. I drop the corner of the shade, afraid of what other faces I might see.

"You come on out, now, ya hear?" The voice belongs to Spudder Rhodes. "Nobody's going to do nothin'. We just got us a few questions."

Rosemary is hunched way over with her arms covering her head. I tap her on the shoulder. "I'm going out there and tell them Eli's sick."

She grabs me and digs her nails into my shoulders so hard I flinch. "Ow!"

"You *can't* go out there. They can't know we're here. If they find out, they'll go after Eli."

"We're nursing him is all."

Rosemary still has a grip on my shoulders. "Two white girls in a colored man's house. You know what they'll do to him?"

I don't want to think about what they'll do. It suddenly occurs to me that Willy might recognize the Green Hornet, although I don't remember Rosemary ever driving it to school. "Where'd you park the car?"

"Out back, behind the house." Rosemary is wearing a thin nightgown. I'm still dressed, but I'm not wearing shoes.

"Get dressed," I tell her. I slip back to the bedroom and put on my sneakers.

Rosemary is pulling on her Bermuda shorts when I come back to the living room.

"Get your things."

She gives me a worried look. "You're not thinking of leaving Eli, are you?"

"Rosemary, you said it yourself. He's going to be in a lot more trouble if the Klan finds us here."

"But they'll break in here. They might hurt him."

"Chances are they'll see he's sick and let him be."

Rosemary throws a fit. She stomps her foot like a stubborn child. "No! We can't do that."

I leave her in the living room and look out the kitchen window. There is a semiwooded area about fifty feet away. If we can get that far, we can hide till the men are gone. Sooner or later, they're going to have to go home.

This is what I'm thinking when I hear a soft tapping at the

back door. It's a polite sort of knock, but urgent. It doesn't sound like somebody is trying to break down the door. My first thought is that it's one of Eli's neighbors come to help. But more than likely they've all bolted their doors and are hiding under their beds.

I peek through a cracked pane of glass in the back door and find myself looking right into Gator's face.

I yank the door open. "Are you crazy, coming here?" I tell him. "Didn't you see half the Klan members in the county parked in Eli's front yard?"

"Where's Eli?" Gator bolts past me. I'm right on his heels. When he spots Rosemary, he stops so fast he almost tips over. They stand there looking at each other for a few seconds; then, without Gator ever saying a word, Rosemary points to Eli's bedroom. Gator ducks through the door and returns with Eli slung over his shoulder like a heavy sack of potatoes. Rosemary and I follow him to the back door.

"Stay low. And keep quiet," Gator says. He points to scruffy thickets of saw palmetto scattered around the back of the house, then points to the woods. "And stay close to the shrubs for cover."

We make our way in between the palmettos as fast as we can. The horns have started up again, blaring their eardrum-shattering honks. And the last thing I see, when I look back, is Eli's lemon tree going up in flames.

23

Julio Gonzalez's wife, Louisa, is bathing Eli's face with a rag she dips in a rusted coffee can filled with water. Louisa's hair is woven into one dark braid that curves along her spine as she bends over Eli. The room is suffocating, hot and cramped.

Another family, the Lopezes, with their five children, shares this place with Julio, Louisa, and their five-week-old son. Two of the Lopez boys, barely school age, sit on a bed with their backs pressed to the wall. They watch Louisa care for Eli. Small clumps of mattress stuffing lie on the floor beneath their bed.

Rosemary sees me staring at the clumps. "Rats," she whispers. "They make nests with it."

I cringe and look over at Julio's baby. He sleeps in an orange crate, nestled in threadbare blankets.

"*¿Está muerto?*" one of the boys says. He points to Eli.

"*Está enfermo,*" Gator tells him. Sick, not dead.

"I'll get some water for Eli to drink," Rosemary says to Gator. She looks around the room, finds an empty jar, and signals me to follow her.

The nearest water tap is next to the camp store. "They've only got three water taps for this whole camp," Rosemary says. "It's downright shameful." She bends over and holds the jar under the faucet. "No hot water at all."

"How did Gator know to come to Eli's?" I've been wanting to ask her this since we got here, but I didn't want to say anything in front of the others. "How come he showed up when he did?"

Rosemary straightens up and looks over at me. "You think these people don't know what's going on around here?"

"What exactly *is* going on?" I'm still not sure. "And why did those men come after Eli tonight? He hasn't done anything. Somehow I don't think not showing up for work for two days would bring the Klan pounding on his door. Travis, maybe. But the whole Klan?"

Rosemary heads back to the Gonzalezes' room. I follow her.

"They probably thought he knew where Gator was."

"Gator was here, wasn't he? Why didn't they just come looking for him here?"

"He hasn't been here since Friday night. After we left the camp."

"Where's he been?"

Rosemary stops walking and looks at me. "Hiding. I'm not sure where."

"Why would he hide?"

"Because the Klan's after him. That's what that meeting you saw was about."

"How do you know that?"

"We just do, okay?"

After all we've been through, I can tell Rosemary still isn't sure whether she can trust me. I don't ask any more questions.

When we get back to the room, she hands Louisa the jar of water. Louisa lifts Eli's head and tries to get him to drink. She dips her finger in the water and runs it over his cracked lips. Eli looks even worse than he did when we first found him. The only doctor I know is Doc Martindale, our family doctor. He's one of those doctors who has two entrances to his office, so I know he treats colored folks. But if I show up at his door in the middle of the night, especially if Dad has the whole town looking for me, the last thing Doc Martindale is going to do is come with me to this camp. Plus there's the problem of how we'd pay him.

I feel totally useless. Discarded mattress stuffing has more purpose than I do right now.

Gator sits at the foot of the bed where Eli is fighting for his life. I can't just stand here doing nothing.

"Gator?" I tap him on the shoulder. "I've got someplace you can hide. Someplace the hounds won't be able to track you down. It's not far from my house."

Rosemary watches me from the bed where she sits with the two Lopez boys. She doesn't say anything, but I can see she's got her guard up.

"Why would I hide?" Gator says. He keeps his eyes on Eli.

"Because the Klan's after you."

Gator shoots a look Rosemary's way. Her expression doesn't change one bit.

"It's two miles back to Benevolence, and then you still have to get to your place," she says to me. "What's that, maybe another two miles? Can you get there before the sun comes up?"

"If we run." I look over at Gator. "Nobody knows this place," I tell him. "I used to play there when I was a kid. It's an old abandoned shack in the swamp about a half mile or so from my house. Nobody ever goes there."

Gator is still looking at Rosemary.

"You should go," she says. "They'll be here soon."

"Come with us," Gator says.

She shakes her head. "I've got to get back to Eli's and get my car. We may need it."

"They'll be checking all the cars coming and going from around here," Gator says. "Probably set up roadblocks."

"They can't keep them up forever," Rosemary tells him.

From the distance we hear the sounds of honking horns. The Klan has left Eli's. They're coming here. "Leave *now*," Rosemary says.

"They can't find *you* here," Gator tells her. "A white girl in a migrant camp for blacks. You know what they'll do?"

"I'm going back to Eli's," she says again. "Go on. Go with Dove."

They look at each other from across the room. I can feel Rosemary's heart beating in my own chest. She is in love with

Gator. And Gator loves her. I can't pretend anymore that they are just friends, that I haven't known this from the first time I saw them together, talking across from the movie theater. I think of Chase and what it was like with us before I found out he was in the Klan. Maybe it's like that for Rosemary and Gator. Only the rest of the world isn't going to see it that way. All they'll see is a colored man and a white woman together. And around these parts, that's just asking to get yourself beat up or maybe even killed.

I turn to Rosemary. "I'll look out for him," I tell her. "I promise."

We slip out the only door and head for the woods. We have to get to the highway and keep as close to it as possible without being seen. We will follow it back to Benevolence, and from there to my dad's groves and beyond to the swamp. A swamp so big people have been lost there and never found.

It has been almost five years since the last time I went to that old shack, a place I first discovered back when I was in third grade. I don't know what we will do if I can't remember the way, or worse, if the shack has crumbled to a heap by now.

We run most of the way. We run like Gator always runs, like the devil is on our heels. We make it to the edge of the swamp while it is still dark. I'm covered with sandspurs again. But I am so scared, I hardly feel their sting.

"You don't want to go in there," Gator says. "Just tell me how to find this place."

I shake my head. "I only know by going. I'll recognize things along the way, but I can't remember them to just tell somebody."

We set off, pushing through the brush. The ground grows soft. Soon I will be up to my knees in swamp water. I take off my sneakers, tie the laces together, and drape them over my shoulders. If I let myself think about the mosquitoes, I will scream. Their buzzing swells in my ears. It's pointless to swat them. There are thousands swarming around us.

I don't bother to tell Gator that those other times I came to the shack, I had a small, flat-bottomed boat I found leaning up against a tree near the edge of the water. Every time I came here, that boat was always there. And since nobody seemed to live anywhere nearby, I borrowed it—lots of times.

But tonight I don't see the boat. I look for it until Gator wants to know what I am doing. "Getting my bearings," I tell him. And then we head off on foot. Gator follows me. It seems like hours, slogging through the water, trying not to get my feet caught in cypress roots and losing my balance, but it has only been a few minutes.

The swamp is so still. There is only the sound of us moving through the water, making little waves. Even the Spanish moss hangs limp and motionless from the cypress branches. The leaves and moss form a canopy. You can't see the stars in this place. No moonlight can get through. Everywhere is the smell of decaying wood.

We are up to our knees in swamp water now. And moving slow.

I don't realize what's happening until Gator swoops me up in his arms. He stands there holding me, staring down at the water. "Cottonmouth," he says. I can feel his heart beating double time.

He doesn't move.

"How much farther?" he asks.

"Not far, a few hundred yards maybe."

"I'll carry you. Just point where we're going." Gator's arms are large and powerful. I don't doubt for a minute he can carry me without much effort. But it wouldn't be right. Me up here, safe against his chest, and him the one who could get bit.

"That'll slow us down," I tell him, sliding out of his arms. "The only way we're going to make it is if we both use our own two feet. Anyway, I'm not afraid of a little old snake." Although the truth is, I am. I'm scared to death of alligators too. But I try not to think about that now.

"If it bites your ankle, it'll swell up with poison," Gator says.

"Well, I know that," I call back to him. I am moving through this water as fast as I can. I am practically running.

It isn't until we are almost to the shack—which, thank goodness, seems to still be in one piece, rusted tin roof and all—that I think about Gator lifting me up like he did. A colored man could get himself hanged for touching a white girl. They would never give Gator time to explain he was just trying to save my life. And even if they did, they more than likely wouldn't give it any consideration.

It is almost dawn when we climb up on the rotting dock. The water is deep here. It forms a large pond. We had to swim the last hundred yards. The space overhead is more open now. I can see a patch of sky turning from gray to pale orange.

Inside the one-room shack is an old rope bed with a stained, lumpy mattress, a wooden table, a couple of chairs made out of tree branches, and an old potbellied stove. Cobwebs hang from every corner. Dust, thick as a piece of card-board, has settled over everything.

"It's not much to look at," I tell Gator.

He laughs at that. Like maybe I thought he was expecting first-class accommodations.

"You'd better rest up before you head back," he says. "I'll keep watch."

Head back? Until now, I haven't even thought about what I'm going to do next. Gator probably thinks I will just go home. But I can't do that. So far all I've managed to do is hop from one place to the next. And somehow, so far, there has been someplace to hop to. I can't help but wonder if I've finally run out of places.

I lie down on the lumpy mattress, thinking I will never sleep again, and just like that, I'm out cold. When I wake up, the sun is hovering above the treetops. Best I can tell, it's early evening. I step out on the narrow porch. Gator is kneeling at the end of the dock. His back is to me and he has his red T-shirt off, washing it in the water. He splashes water on his face and over his head, on his chest and arms. With the sunlight spilling through the tree branches onto his strong back, his skin glows a warm maple-syrup brown.

I know I shouldn't be watching him, but I can't seem to help it. He sits back, wrings out the shirt, and turns side-ways to spread it on the dock to dry. That's when I see what Rosemary has seen all along, that Gator is good-looking, *real* good-looking. I never noticed before. He has always been . . . well . . . just Gator.

I step back inside the shack, embarrassed about thinking of him like that.

For a while I sit on the musty mattress, watching a spider weaving a web in the corner of the window. It stops weaving long enough to tend to a fly that's just got itself tangled up in the web. The spider's setting up house and doing its grocery shopping at the same time. Very efficient. You can only watch something like that for so long, and then sooner or later you are going to have to visit what is going on inside your head, including the things you would rather not think about. Things like where your next meal is going to come from.

Two days ago I had three balanced meals a day. I had a bedroom with curtains and a matching bedspread. I had a father who loved me and took care of me and made sure I got my allowance every week. I had Delia, who has been the only mother I have ever really known. I had friends. And I had Chase. Right now I can't be sure what I have or don't have. All because I couldn't let things be. All because I couldn't accept the way things are in Benevolence. Is this what Emily Dickinson meant about remorse being "the Adequate of Hell"?

When Gator comes inside a short time later, he says, "You'd better get on back. Your daddy's going to wonder where you got to. They've probably been out looking for you since yesterday morning."

I don't say anything.

Gator's shirt is still damp. He has a handful of white chunks—swamp cabbage. He drops a few of them in my lap and puts the rest on the dusty table. I eat them raw, even though the taste is a little bitter. I am so hungry I could eat the bark off a tree.

"How'd you get this?" I ask him. Swamp cabbage is the center of a young palm tree. You have to chop the palm down with an ax, then cut away the stalk to get to the heart. You don't just tear it apart with your bare hands.

Gator steps outside and comes back in with a rusty ax. "Found this out back by the woodpile." He sets the ax over by the potbellied stove.

"There's probably brim in that pond. I'll try to rig up something to catch a few. Cottonmouths make pretty good eating too. Maybe I'll catch us one." He grins over at me. He picks up a chunk of swamp cabbage, wipes the dust off on his shirt, and bites into it.

"Why's the Klan after you?" I ask.

Gator pulls one of the chairs away from the table and sits in it backward, the way Chase did that day in the cafeteria. It seems like years ago, me and Chase talking about the pickers while he kept snitching bites of my meat loaf. But it's only been about a week and a half.

"Travis, he's mad as hell because I'm trying to help the pickers get what's fair. He's been cheating them long enough. I thought it was time we did something about that."

"Travis killed Gus Washburn," I say.

Gator runs his thumb along his upper lip a few times, like he's thinking about something. "Yeah. I heard about that."

"How? I only told Delia about it yesterday morning."

"Bad news travels fast around here. When the pickers heard about Gus, not a single one of them would get on Travis's truck yesterday. Probably didn't this morning either. Don't know that for a fact, since I wasn't there. Travis, he's blaming me, saying I put them up to it."

"Did you?"

"What, getting them to not show up after they heard about

Gus?" He shakes his head. "They did that on their own." A grin eases across Gator's face. "But I got them to agree to a slowdown, not working as fast as they should, not picking as much fruit. Some of the pickers took turns not showing up. It was starting to hit Travis where it hurts the most. In his wallet.

"At first everybody was scared Travis would just pick out a new crew. But all that's left over in Winter Hill are a few lazy stoop laborers. They don't know the first thing about picking citrus. Travis, he'd lose even more time training them.

"We had to get everybody in the camp to agree to the slowdown, otherwise it wouldn't work. Travis made it harder by threatening to turn in some of the illegals who don't have work visas. But he knows he can get in trouble for bringing them over the border in the first place."

Finally it's beginning to make sense, what Rosemary meant when she said Travis probably thought Eli was part of the slowdown.

"By yesterday afternoon word was all over Benevolence that Travis killed Gus Washburn," Gator says. "But white folks, they don't care. They think Travis is going to keep the lid on us troublemakers. Travis and the rest of the Klan have all the white folks scared half to death thinking the pickers are going to burn their houses down over their heads. Every little Girl Scout campfire that gets out of hand, we're getting blamed for it." Gator laughs just thinking about that. "Travis, he's making sure everybody thinks it was one of the pickers who set the fires, any fire at all, doesn't matter which fire. And the white folks, they believe him. Doesn't matter what he did in the past—killed a black man, cheated his crew, made slaves out of the immigrants he brought in—none of that matters, because Travis, he's gonna keep law and order in this town. That's how they see it."

I've never seen Gator this angry before. Right now the air in this tiny room is practically crackling with his rage, the way wood crackles when it's on fire. It scares me a little, seeing him this way. But I don't let on.

It looks to me like Travis is trying to make an example of Gator. He's probably thinking if he does, the other pickers will back off. He thinks they'll be too afraid to pull any more slowdowns or not show up for work. I don't blame Gator one bit for being mad. And I'm starting to worry about Travis figuring out who told Delia about his killing Gus in the first place, and about what he'll do if he ever gets his hands on that person.

Gator gets up and looks out the door. "Sun's behind the trees, better get going."

"I can't go home," I tell him. "And I don't have anyplace else to go."

His back is still to me when he says, "Your daddy probably has half the state of Florida out looking for you. If they find you here, you know what they'll do."

"They won't find us," I say.

"They'll use the hounds."

"We came here through swamp water. It's like I said before, the dogs can't track that."

"They'll follow the scent to the place we went into the water. They'll know we're in the swamp somewhere. Your daddy'll have them cutting down trees. He won't stop looking for you until there's not a cypress left standing."

I know he's right, but I don't move from the bed.

Gator looks over at me. We don't say anything more about it after that. For a while, we don't talk at all. Gator wanders around the shack, inspecting every seam, every crack. He opens the potbellied stove, sifts around in the ashes, and pulls out a piece of burnt wood.

He goes outside and a few minutes later comes back with some leafy branches, which he uses to sweep the dust from the table. This whole time I am trying to gag down the last of the swamp cabbage.

Gator sits down at the table and begins working that piece of burnt wood. Every so often he looks over at me. That's how I know he's drawing my picture. So I stay put. In my head I recite lines from poems. I don't remember whole poems, but I remember some of my favorite stanzas. It keeps my mind occupied.

After a while Gator slides his chair back and studies the picture he drew of me on the top of the table. Right about then the door to the shack flies open with a bang.

24

Chase Tully's body blocks the light coming through the doorway. And the first thing that pops into my head is that he is bone dry. However he got himself here, it wasn't by wading through the water or swimming through the pond. The second thing is, I suddenly remember bringing him to this place once before, years ago, when I was maybe nine or ten. How could I have forgotten that?

Chase's face is in shadow. I can't read his expression.

I am having those Keatsian fears of ceasing to be—*again*. My heart is thudding in my ears. If Chase is here, so is the Klan. Or they are going to be real soon.

He looks from me to Gator and back to me again. He's

wearing his leather jacket, singed sleeves, scorch marks, and all. I stand up so fast, I almost lose my balance. "So help me, if you've brought the Klan here"—I point to the ax by the potbellied stove—"I'll hack you into little pieces and throw them to the alligators."

Chase steps inside the door where I can see him a little better. He gives me his lazy grin.

I look over at Gator. I'm waiting for him to do something, wrestle Chase to the floor so we can tie him up. Maybe bash his brains in. But Gator just goes back to his drawing. "We've got to get out of here," I tell him.

Chase slips his hands into his jacket pockets, walks over to the table, and studies the drawing Gator is working on. He looks over at me, then back at the picture. "Good likeness," he says. "You really captured her ornery side."

"Gator!" I shout.

"Dove's right," Chase says. "They're not far behind me. We gotta go."

We? Like comets roaring through space, a hundred questions zip through my mind. But there's no time to ask. Chase and Gator are out the door and heading down to the end of the dock. I'm right behind them. Tied to the post is the flat-bottomed boat I couldn't find earlier. More questions. Still no time. We climb into the boat. Gator takes the pole.

Chase shows Gator which way to go. I have no idea where he is taking us. Best I can tell from the little daylight left is that we are heading northwest. I have never gone farther than the shack before. For all I know, the Klan will be waiting for us when we get to wherever we're going. So why isn't Gator saying anything?

"It was you, wasn't it?" I say to Chase's back. It's the middle of May and a regular steam bath out here, but he hasn't taken off that jacket.

"Me what?" he says over his shoulder.

"You're the one who warned Gator what was going on, so he'd go into hiding. And you told him about the Klan going over to Eli's place last night. Didn't you?"

He doesn't say anything. Neither does Gator. They don't have to. I know I'm right.

It makes sense now, Chase not helping Gator the day Willy and Earl beat him up. Not flat out calling Willy a liar when he spread those rumors about our barn. Going with his dad to the Klan meeting. It all adds up. He couldn't let on to his dad and Willy and the others. If they got suspicious—if they figured it out—Chase wouldn't have been able to help Gator and the others because he'd probably be in a full body cast by now—or worse.

"Where'd you find this boat?" I ask.

"Where I hid it."

"Hid it? Why?"

He swats at a mosquito on his neck. "A couple years back I figured if I didn't hide it, somebody might come along and take it." He angles his body so he can look at my face. "After you showed me this place, I used to come out here sometimes, do a little fishing."

"How'd you know to look for me here?"

Chase just smiles and shakes his head, like he expects I should know the answer to that. He turns his back to me again.

After a while we come to a small inlet. The bank slopes up to woods. Chase tells Gator to steer the boat into the inlet. Between the two of them, they carry it up to the woods and hide it behind some bushes. We follow Chase along a narrow, overgrown path. He takes off his jacket and ties the sleeves around his waist.

After a short time we come to an open field. The sun has gone down, and the sky is a dusty pink. Across the meadow are orange trees. I know this place. We are at the far end of the Tully property.

"Are you crazy?" I say.

"This is the last place they'll look for you," Chase says. "We'll wait until it's dark. Then we'll head back toward the main house." He looks over at Gator. "There's a smokehouse nobody's used for years. You can stay in there until I figure out how to get you out of the county. Right now they've got roadblocks up all over the place. They think you kidnapped Dove. At least that's what Travis Waite's got 'em thinking."

"Does my dad think that too?" I ask.

"I haven't seen your dad since Friday night," Chase says.

"If they've got the hounds out looking for Gator," I say, "they'll track him here to the smokehouse."

"The hounds only took them as far as the edge of the swamp," Chase says. "They lost the scent."

"You were with them?"

"It was the best way for me to find out if they were on your trail, so I could warn you. As soon as I saw them go into the swamp, I knew where you were."

We wait until the sky turns violet gray. Chase leads us along the edge of the woods to the groves nearest the Tully house. We stay among the orange trees until we aren't far from the barn. "That's it over there," Chase says to Gator. He points to a wooden building with a smokestack on top. "The door's not locked."

Gator tails after Chase. I stay close behind them both, keeping an eye out in case anybody is following us.

The smokehouse has a dirt floor. Even though it has been years since this place was used to smoke meat and fish, the pungent odor of hickory smoke still clings to the blackened walls.

"Dove and me will get you some food and water," Chase tells Gator. "And a blanket."

Gator looks around, then sits down on the damp dirt. "Thanks."

"I should stay here too," I tell Chase. "If they've been out looking for me, what are your mom and dad going to think, me showing up at your place?"

"Nobody's home. My dad's out searching for Gator with the others. Mom's been up in Tallahassee all week visiting Aunt May."

So nobody is more surprised than Chase when we are standing in the kitchen making peanut butter sandwiches for Gator and Jacob Tully comes barreling through the back door like an angry stallion busting out of his corral.

He looks from Chase to me, then turns back to Chase. "Where is he?" he barks.

Chase gives his father a blank stare. "Who?"

In the distance I hear the howls of the bloodhounds. They are on to the scent. Gator's scent. The blasting horns aren't far behind. I run out the back door in time to see Gator tearing out of the smokehouse. The men on foot, the ones with the dogs, are only about a hundred yards behind him. A parade of pickups and cars winds through the Tullys' backyard.

There don't seem to be as many as there were over at Eli's place. But I don't get my hopes up. It's possible that only some of the men have come back with Jacob. The others might still be out there, looking someplace else.

Travis, Jimmy, Moss, and Spudder are in the lead like some twisted version of the Four Horsemen of the Apocalypse. They act like they're on some sacred mission. And they are the most terrifying sight I have ever set eyes on.

They surround the smokehouse and shine their lights toward the woods, where I see two of the dogs lunge at Gator just as he gets to the first line of trees.

"Chase!" I yell. But he doesn't come. I am scared to death for Gator. He has got to be thinking Chase led him into a trap, that he lied to us. I know that's what's going through Gator's mind, because that's what's going through mine. I only hope he doesn't think I was in on it.

I slam open the back door and find Jacob Tully standing over his son. Chase lies on the floor with a bleeding lip.

"You better make up your mind whose side you're on, boy. And *fast*!" Jacob pounds his fist into the palm of his other hand. Pounds and pounds and keeps on pounding. I expect him to start in on Chase's face again, but he doesn't. When he realizes I'm there, he barks, "Your daddy is looking all over creation for you." And *bam!* he's out the door.

● ● ● ● ● ● ● ● ● ● ● ● ● ● ● ●

"They've got Gator," I tell Chase.

I run cold water onto a dish towel and try to wash the blood from his mouth. But he pushes my hand away.

"I know where they'll take him," he says. He staggers to his feet. We get to the back porch as the last truck is pulling out of the yard. Chase heads straight for the T-bird. I climb in the passenger side.

"Stay here," he says.

I shake my head. "No."

"Dove, this is too dangerous. You have no idea what they're—"

"I'm not getting out of this car." I reach over and turn the key in the ignition. "We're wasting time."

"Promise me you'll stay in the car, then, when we get there."

I don't say anything. I'm thinking about how I broke my last promise, after Chase made me swear not to tell anybody about Travis killing Gus.

"Promise, or I'm going to pull you right out of this car and lock you in the smokehouse."

"Okay, okay." I mumble. "Just let's go."

I don't have to ask Chase where we're going. I already know. To the place where the Klan holds its meetings. To Spudder Rhodes's house.

"Why did your dad come back to the house?" I ask. "Did the hounds lead him and the others there?"

Chase shrugs. "I don't know. Maybe he got suspicious when I suddenly disappeared from the search. He knows you and I are friends." He looks over at me. "We are, aren't we? Still friends?"

I swallow hard. "Course we are," I whisper. It is on the tip of my tongue to say we're more than that. But I don't.

"Maybe he came back for some other reason and saw my

car there. Or maybe he's suspected for a while that I wasn't exactly Klan material and he's been keeping an eye on me. Who knows how his mind works? I sure as hell don't."

"How long you been pretending to be in the Klan?"

Chase draws a deep breath and lets it out. "My dad started dragging me along last year. Not to all the meetings. Just a few—maybe three."

"And you been helping Gator and the others all this time?"

"Look . . . Dove . . . I don't want to spoil this Chase the Hero thing you got going on in your head at the moment, but up until picking season started last March there wasn't any need to help Gator or anybody else. The Klan's never been all that active around here, not since back in the twenties. Most of the men you saw at the meeting last week aren't even members. They're just worried about what's been going on with the pickers—afraid there's going to be some kind of uprising or something."

We turn down the dirt road leading to Spudder's house. "You remember a couple years ago, when those colored kids wanted to go to that all-white high school in Little Rock?"

"You mean when President Eisenhower had to send in the National Guard to protect them?"

Chase nods. "Some of the folks around here are worried that the government is going to try to run their lives—use the military to make them do things they don't want to, like letting colored kids go to white schools. The Klan's been cashing in on those worries, and not just around here.

"Then Gator started organizing the pickers, telling them about strikes and slowdowns and the like. Travis, he's been out to get Gator for years. He's always hated that he couldn't control him. The slowdowns just gave Travis an excuse to go after him. He got his friends, some of them Klan members like himself, to back him up."

We are heading across the meadow to the meeting place I found over a week ago. "It sounds to me like this is Travis's personal vigilante group."

"Yeah, well. He's the one who's been stirring 'em up, that's for sure."

We are driving down the narrow road that leads to where the Klan meets. Suddenly the glaring lightbulbs from the cross flash on. Chase doesn't pull into the lot where the other pickups and cars are parked. Instead he leaves the T-bird by the side of the road, about two hundred yards from the cinder-block building and trailer where all the men have gathered. Gator isn't anywhere in sight.

"What are they going to do to him?"

Chase presses both hands against the dashboard and stares straight ahead. "Anything they can think of," he says.

"How come they're not wearing their robes and hoods?"

"I've never seen them wear robes," he says. "Maybe they don't even have them. But if they do and they're not wearing them, that's a bad sign."

"Why is that a bad sign?"

"If they're just going to rough somebody up, they'd probably wear robes. That way, if the person tries to press charges, he can't say for sure he recognized any faces."

"He could say he recognized the voices."

"Doesn't hold up in court. That's the point." Chase has his back to me. He's watching the men across the road.

"They wouldn't kill Gator, would they? They wouldn't go that far?" My heart has started to pound like a basketball someone is driving down the court at full speed. Billy Tyler's horrible picture of the colored man hanging from the tree, eyes bulging, staring at nothing, has crept back into my head. I am trying not to panic.

Chase shrugs. "All I know is they were planning to make an example of him, send a message to the other pickers."

I dig my fingers into his arm. "We can't let anything happen to Gator. We've got to do something."

"*We* aren't doing anything," he says. Chase unlocks my shaking hand from his arm and presses it against his cheek, then kisses my sweaty palm. "You promised to stay in the car, remember?" He opens his door and climbs out. His jacket is still around his waist. He unties it, and the way he puts it back on, it's as if he's getting ready for battle. He pulls the keys from the ignition and tosses them to me. They land in my lap. "If things turn ugly, get out of here. Fast!"

I don't have a chance to ask him what qualifies as "ugly" because he is already crossing the road, heading toward the woods on the outskirts of the open field. It looks as if he is planning to circle around behind the cinder-block building.

Across the way the men have gathered outside. They seem to be waiting for something. Some have shotguns. Some are holding rifles.

A few minutes later the door flies open. Travis Waite and Spudder Rhodes step outside. They have Gator between them. They stand on the steps, looking out over all the faces. Best I can tell from this distance, Gator's hands are tied behind his back. He has to be scared out of his wits. My whole body is shaking now. I can barely take a breath, my chest is so tight.

The men fall back, leaving a narrow opening for the three of them to walk through. Spudder and Travis shove Gator along in front of them. Some of the men stab burning cigarettes at Gator, in his face, on his head, his arms. Gator kicks at their legs, swings his broad shoulders, and throws his body at them. He knocks a few of the men off balance.

I send frantic mental messages to Chase. *Hurry. Hurry. You have to stop this.* I look for him, but I don't see him.

I can't just sit here and do nothing. I made Rosemary a promise to look out for Gator. My promise to Chase to stay put doesn't seem real important right now. I get out of the car and make my way across the road to the field, to where the glaring cross is so bright it almost looks like daylight out, to where these men are burning Gator with their cigarettes. And I don't doubt for a minute that this is just the beginning.

I climb in the back of somebody's pickup and peer over the roof. There are fewer cars and trucks here than there were at Eli's, even fewer than there were at the Tully place when they came to get Gator. From where I am, I count eight. There aren't as many men either. Only about fifteen. It seems a lot of folks have dropped out along the way. Maybe they have decided they don't have the stomach for this ugliness and have gone on home.

I look for my dad, but I don't see him.

Travis Waite and Spudder Rhodes are tying Gator to the telephone pole below the lighted cross. They pull his arms around the pole and tie his hands behind it. They bind his feet. I am worried sick about what's going to happen.

"Maybe you want to say a few words to the boys, here, before we get started?" Travis says to Gator.

Gator looks Travis square in the eyes but doesn't say anything.

"Cat got your tongue, nigger?"

Gator has still got his eyes on Travis. Travis wallops him across the face with his fist.

I hear a muffled grunt coming from Gator, but he doesn't yell out. He doesn't say a word.

"Tell you what, nigger. You apologize to everybody here for all those fires you set and maybe we'll consider letting you go." Travis's laugh sounds like a bull snorting.

Gator says, "Everybody here knows most of those fires were caused by lightning. Or they were accidents. Nobody set 'em."

Travis takes another punch at him. He looks around at the other men. "Anybody else want to take a crack at this jigaboo?"

Moss Henley breaks from the mob, slinging those bulldog shoulders of his, slipping off his belt while he's walking. He tears Gator's red T-shirt right off his body. The belt buckle catches Gator across the eye and then the chest. I feel it coming down on me. I feel the thud of metal on the side of my face. I hear it in my ears.

Travis shoves Moss aside. He gets right in Gator's face. "You cost me my job, you damn nigger!" he yells. "You got me fired. My crew doesn't show up for two days, and I lose my job. You think you aren't gonna have to pay for that?"

"Your crew didn't show up because they found out you killed Gus Washburn," Gator says.

I can't believe he's talking back to Travis like that. It's like throwing gasoline on a fire. I am scared to death for Gator.

Spudder steps out of the crowd and moseys up to Gator. "Travis's employment problems aside, boy, we got us a more important matter. Concerning the whereabouts of Lucas Alderman's daughter."

Dead silence. They are all waiting to hear what Gator has to say about this.

"Now, a few of the boys here"—Spudder nods to the others—"they found this picture in a shack out back of Lucas's place. In the swamp, right, boys?" Some of the men nod. "A picture drawn on some old table. Fresh drawn, they tell me." Spudder tugs at his lower lip while he slowly paces back and forth in front of Gator. "Now, Travis here, he tells me you're always drawing."

"On the job," Travis yells to the others. "When he's supposed to be working."

"He's seen your pictures," Spudder says, not missing a beat. "And he says you done this one. The one on the table. That true, boy?"

Gator just stares him down.

"Uh-huh. Well, now, to hear the boys here tell it, that picture's the exact likeness of Dove Alderman, the missing girl in question. Now, I don't know about you, but it surely does look to me like the two of you were in that shack together. Am I right?"

Gator doesn't so much as blink.

"So we're all thinking maybe you took that poor little girl from her home. Maybe kidnapped her to get back at her daddy for keeping Travis on all these years. Now, that's assuming you believe all those lies going around about how Gus Washburn got himself killed." He stops pacing, spreads his legs for balance, and hooks his thumbs in his belt. He's wearing his gun. He looks Gator in the eyes. "Does that sound about right to you?"

Gator doesn't say a word.

"Then there's this other matter of a bag we found at Eli's place. Seems it had Dove Alderman's school books and all in it. So we're thinking maybe you got Eli to help you hide your victim. That being Miss Alderman, of course. I guess that makes him an accessory to the crime, now, doesn't it?"

My duffel bag! I'd forgotten all about it. Now they will surely go after Eli too. *Where the hell is Chase?* I look around but don't see him.

Gator is still not talking.

Spudder says, "Well, maybe the boys here can help jog that memory of yours." He steps back and Moss comes in swinging that belt again, until Jimmy Wheeler grabs it out of Moss's hand. For one hopeful minute I think he's going to make Moss stop. But then Jimmy takes a crack at Gator himself. Two more men come forward, swinging belts. I shove my fist in my mouth to keep from yelling out.

The belts crash down on Gator. I taste blood in my mouth and realize I've bitten into my knuckle.

That's when I see Chase coming from around the side of the cinder-block building. Slowly he makes his way up to the back of the crowd. The men don't notice him, which I'm pretty sure is what he was counting on.

They are shouting, "Get him good, Jimmy!" Shouting, "Beat the crap out of him!" Shouting, "Kill the nigger!" Their voices rise into the hot night air. Gator's chin drops to his chest. I can't tell if his eyes are closed because there is so much blood. Blood runs from his head, from his chest, from his arms. He is bathed in red. I am shaking all over. But I can't let this nightmare go on for another minute. I have to tell them that Gator didn't kidnap me. That I'm fine.

I start to climb down from the pickup just as Chase steps out of the crowd.

He walks up to Jimmy and takes the belt. He says, loud enough for them to hear him over in the next county, "I think Gator's had about enough, don't you?"

The men stop their shouting and whooping and laughing. They stare at Chase with glazed eyes. They look at the belt in his hand, expecting him to use it like the son of a respected Klansman should. They are waiting for him to draw more blood.

But Chase throws the belt on the ground. "Dove Alderman is fine. Gator didn't kidnap her and my father knows it. He saw Dove and me together in my kitchen not more than a half hour ago." He turns away and starts to untie Gator from the telephone pole.

Travis grabs Chase by the arm, spins him around, and lands his fist right in his face. The back of Chase's head bounces off the telephone pole.

Jacob Tully shoves aside two men and steps forward. In the glare of that lit-up cross, I can see that his face is red with rage. I'm expecting him to beat the tar out of Travis for hitting Chase.

The two of them stand there—Jacob and Travis—exchanging looks. Jacob turns to the mob. He takes in all their faces. He swings around to confront Chase. "Looks to me like you've made your choice, boy. Now you're gonna have to live with it." His head is bobbing up and down, like this is about what he expected. Then he says to Jimmy, "Tie this nigger lover up with his friend here."

It's like I'm seeing Jacob yank Chase from that tractor and dislocate his shoulder all over again. I'm so stunned I can't think straight.

Jimmy looks from Jacob to Chase, raises his hands like somebody has yelled "Put 'em up," shakes his head, and takes a step back. Not Travis. He grabs Chase's arms. Chase breaks away and lands a few good punches on Travis's face before two other men come running up and grab him. They tie him to the other side of the pole. He and Gator can't see each other, but their hands press against each other's backs. Some of the other men exchange worried looks. I can tell they don't like the way things are going.

Travis whirls his belt above his head a few times like a lasso and takes a crack at Chase. I can't let this happen. There isn't a doubt in my mind that if this goes on much longer, these men will end up killing Gator and Chase.

I climb down from the pickup and shove my way through smelly, sweaty bodies. The men step aside, startled. When I'm almost to the open space where Chase and Gator are tied to the pole, somebody shouts, "Hey, it's Lucas's girl. She's here." Whoever's doing the shouting, I can tell he's darn relieved to see me.

I step into the open circle like a boxer climbing into the ring. For a minute nobody moves. They don't know what to make of my being here. They aren't sure what to do with me.

"It's like Chase said, nobody kidnapped me," I tell them. "I'm fine. Gator's innocent. So you can stop this belt-whipping right now."

Willy Podd steps out from behind his dad, Macon. He saunters up to us like he's in no hurry. When he gets about two feet from me, he leans forward and spits right in my face. "Nigger lover," he says.

I wipe off the glob of spit. "Let them go," I say, turning to Travis. "Or I'm going straight to the state police."

Travis laughs. I can smell the liquor on his breath. He's laughing so hard, tears are running down his face. They leave dirty streaks on his cheeks. A few of the other men laugh too, like this is the best joke they've heard in years. But most of them can't even look me in the eye.

Chase shouts at me to get on home. I can tell by his voice he's mad as hell at me. Moss Henley laces into Chase with the belt.

All I'm doing is making things worse.

"Tie her up with her friends," Willy says. "She's the reason Travis got fired, her going around telling lies about him, saying he killed Gus Washburn."

Travis snaps up some rope that's lying near the base of the pole. The look he gives me is terrifying. Hard as I try, I can't find even the tiniest hint of humanity in that face.

Somewhere in the back of my mind it is beginning to sink in that my father has fired Travis. And Travis knows I told Delia he killed Gus, and he's blaming Gator for the pickers not showing up, blaming both of us for getting him fired.

Jacob Tully comes forward and takes the rope from Travis. "We don't lay a hand on Lucas's daughter. Understand?"

"Where the hell *is* Lucas, anyway?" Travis says, looking around. "Everybody's supposed to be here tonight."

Travis doesn't seem to have noticed that a lot of folks have deserted his ranks along the way.

Jacob glares at me. His face is like chiseled stone. My mouth is so dry I can't swallow. "He went out looking for his daughter. Said he wasn't going to stop till he found her."

"Well, she's right here," Willy says. "Where Lucas should be."

Jacob signals two of the men to keep an eye on me. To make sure I don't cause any trouble. He says he is going to personally deliver me to my dad when they are done with Chase and Gator.

Travis has disappeared for a few minutes, but now he's cutting through the mob, swinging an ax. He stands in front of Gator. "I've decided to cut you loose, nigger. How's that? I'm gonna chop those ropes right off. Course, I've never been real good with an ax. I might miss." Travis holds the ax handle in one hand, swinging it like a golf club. "That happens, well, you might lose a hand or two. Won't be able to make any more of those pretty pictures of yours. But don't pay that no mind. You're gonna be free."

I hear whispers and mumblings among the men. Even Jacob Tully is starting to look worried.

The two men guarding me are so busy watching what Travis is going to do that I break away from them with no effort at all. I run over and grab the ax right out of Travis's hand before he knows what hit him. I stand in front of Gator, holding up that ax, knowing that any second this mob of men will be all over us. They won't stop until the three of us are buzzard food.

Somewhere in the distance I hear car horns blasting. More Klan folks. Probably the ones who were at Eli's earlier are just now catching up.

My heart is racing so fast I'm getting light-headed.

I don't want to watch them coming for us. I don't want to see what's going to happen next. It's all I can do not to close my eyes. To shut it all out. But I don't dare.

Chase's voice drifts over to me. "Dove, drop the ax. They aren't going to do anything to you."

"I can't," I tell him. "If they get the ax they'll chop you and Gator to pieces." I am shaking so bad, I'm afraid my knees will buckle. But I hold on to that ax.

"Drop it," he says.

By now my grip on the handle is so tight, I couldn't let go if I wanted.

My heart pounds in my ears. The thudding dulls the noise from the honking horns as it grows louder. The men begin shuffling their feet, looking over their shoulders, staring at each other. They shake their heads. They don't know what's going on either.

The horns are followed by the glare of headlights. Nobody moves. We stand there watching as battered old pickups and cars rumble into the field. They form a circle around all of us, facing inward. The high beams are so bright, the men have to shade their eyes. I squint, keeping a tight grip on the ax.

I hear a car door slam shut and look up to see Delia coming straight at me. She is carrying the biggest kitchen knife I have ever laid eyes on. Rosemary Howell is right behind her. Other car doors slam. With the headlights shining in my eyes,

I can't see their faces, but somehow I know some of our pickers are out there.

Delia doesn't have to shove her way through the men like I did. They see that knife and get out of her way. She walks past them like she doesn't fear a thing, like she's got nothing to lose. She steps right up to Travis Waite and holds that knife just a few inches from his throat. Except for his Adam's apple bouncing up and down, Travis doesn't move. He doesn't breathe.

We all wait to see if Delia is really going to use that knife on him.

"I'm going to cut those boys loose," Delia tells him. "You try to stop me, and I'll have to kill you. Like you did Gus. There's not a whole lot standing between you and this knife right now except common decency."

Travis lets out a sick little chuckle. I can tell he's afraid of what Delia might do if her common decency should suddenly slip.

From behind the men comes the sound of shotguns being cocked. The Klan members fire nervous looks at each other. They have just figured out Delia isn't the only one who has come here armed tonight. They clutch their shotguns and rifles to their chests. They are sitting ducks in these headlights and they know it.

Rosemary is trying to untie Gator. But the blood makes the ropes slippery. It's all over her hands.

Delia takes the knife and saws through the ropes, the whole time keeping an eye on Travis. I hold up the ax like I just might have to use it on him if he takes one step toward Delia.

Gator's body slides down the pole, landing in a heap at the base. Delia cuts Chase loose. Then she slips her hands beneath Gator's armpits and pulls him toward the line of cars. I take a step forward and reach for Gator's legs to help her. Delia's kitchen knife looks like it's growing out of Gator's armpit. She shoves it toward me and the look on her face stops me cold. It tells me if I take one step closer she won't hesitate to use that knife on me or anybody else who gets in her way.

It feels as if Delia's knife has gone straight through my heart.

Delia and Rosemary manage to get Gator into the back-seat of Rosemary's old Ford. They pull out. The others stay behind. They keep their headlights aimed right at the Klan, daring any of them to make a move. Travis and his friends will probably try to find a way to make them pay for this later, even though they can't see who's out there. These folks know that too. But I guess they've had about enough of this business because they're not backing down. For now, anyway, they've got this small group of Klansmen outnumbered.

"Are you okay to walk?" I say to Chase. Except for the split lip Jacob gave him earlier, a swollen eye, and a gash on his cheek from somebody's belt, he doesn't look too bad.

"Yeah, I can walk."

I pick up Gator's torn T-shirt from the ground by the telephone pole. "Then we need to follow Delia," I tell him. "We have to find out where they're taking Gator."

● ● ● ● ● ● ● ● ● ● ● ● ● ● ● ●

Chase lets me drive the T-bird. That's how I know he is hurting a lot worse than he's letting on. We stay a few car lengths behind Rosemary. When we reach Benevolence, Rosemary heads for the colored quarters. "They're taking Gator to Delia's place," I tell Chase.

When I pull up in front of Delia's, Chase says he'll wait for me in the car.

I knock on the front door but no one answers. The door is unlocked. I slip inside and stand in Delia's living room. I clutch Gator's red shirt against my chest. Muffled voices float down the hall. "Delia?" I call.

But it is Rosemary who appears in front of one of the doors off the hallway. "Best if you went on home, Dove," she whispers.

I go as far as the bedroom door. "I need to know if Gator's going to be all right."

Rosemary crosses her arms and rubs them hard with her hands, as if she's freezing to death. She takes a few steps toward me. "We don't know. It looks bad. Real bad. He's lost a lot of blood." She glances back over her shoulder. "Delia's tending to him."

"What about Eli?"

"His fever broke. I think he's going to be okay. Louisa is taking good care of him."

I am relieved for Eli, but I'm worried sick about Gator.

Rosemary takes me gently by the arm and steers me back into the living room. "Those men could've killed you tonight."

"But then you showed up." I smile at her. "Like the cavalry in some old western."

Rosemary smiles too. "Lucky you."

"How'd you know where to find us?"

"You," Rosemary says.

"Me?"

"The other morning when you came to Luellen's, when you told me about your daddy and Chase, you said the night before you'd been over to Spudder Rhodes's place where the Klan was meeting.

"As soon as word got out about Travis killing Gus Washburn, the pickers, they decided they didn't want to work for a crew boss who was a murderer. They knew Travis was going to go after Gator. Everybody knew it. So instead of showing up for work Saturday and Sunday, they were out rounding up some of the pickers from other camps to join them in case Gator needed help. Except none of them knew where Spudder's place was. So I went looking for Delia, hoping she'd know."

"I was wrong about Chase being in the Klan."

Rosemary nods. "I know." She looks down the hall at the light coming from the open bedroom door. "Delia didn't know where Spudder lived, either. But then she got a phone call about how the Klan had Gator. And the person she talked to told her where to find him."

"A call from who?" I ask.

Rosemary seems to be studying the photographs on the wall. "Somebody called Delia and told her. That's all I know."

"Here," I say, handing her Gator's shirt. "He's going to need this." Before Rosemary can stop me, I head back down the hall to the room where Delia is nursing Gator. She looks up when I come through the door. She is holding a blood-soaked towel. A basin of dark pink water sits on a wooden chair by the bed. This is Jeremiah's room. I can tell by the pictures of Negro baseball players all over the wall.

Gator's face is swollen and bleeding. It could be Gus lying there, the night Travis hit him with that car. Delia has got to be reliving that whole nightmare over in her mind.

"Didn't Rosemary tell you to get on home?" she asks.

"How's Gator?"

"Bad."

"Is he going to live?"

"Only the Lord knows the answer to that one." She stands up, pressing her hand against her back. "How's that Tully boy?"

"He's going to be okay. He's outside in his car."

"Well, don't keep him waiting."

"Delia—"

"Your daddy's been everywhere looking for you. He's not going to rest till you get yourself back home."

"How do you know that?"

"He was here, first thing this morning. You weren't gone but a half hour when he shows up." Delia wrings out a washcloth in the pink water and presses it gently on Gator's swollen face. I stare hard at his chest, trying to see if he's still breathing. He is, but his breathing is shallow.

"My dad was here? He came *here*?" I don't know why I'm so surprised by this. It makes sense, seeing as how I told him the night before I was going to tell Delia about Travis.

"He wanted to know if you'd been here or telephoned. I told him you'd been here, all right. And I said you told me about Travis Waite killing Gus. Your daddy, he tries to make it better, saying he's sorry and that he only wanted to protect me and Jeremiah, that he only wanted to look after me. I said I didn't need nobody looking after me, what I needed was Travis Waite in jail."

I sit down on the edge of the bed and take Gator's hand. It is cool and dry. "Come on, Gator," I tell him. "This fight is just beginning. You can't walk away now." I press his hand to my cheek. I hold it in my lap while Delia puts iodine on his wounds and bandages them.

Maybe I'm looking for any hopeful sign I can get, but I imagine I feel his hand give mine a light squeeze. I squeeze his back.

"Rosemary said somebody called you, told you the Klan had Gator and where you'd probably find him."

Delia is patting the welts on Gator's chest with the damp washcloth. She looks over at me. "It was your daddy who phoned me."

I swear I feel Gator's hand twitch in mine.

"Dad? My dad warned you?" I can't seem to wrap my mind around this piece of news. It's too much to think about right now.

"Your daddy, yes. And you'd better get on home to him right now. He's worried sick."

I'm not ready to go home yet. I'm not ready to face my dad. "Let me stay here and help," I say.

"Haven't you done about enough helping for a while?"

My vision starts to blur, but I blink back my tears. "I could've done what my dad did, tried to keep you from being hurt, never telling you the truth. Are you going to hate me for the rest of your life for telling you about Travis?"

Delia looks surprised when I say this. "I don't hate you, child." She rests her hands on her hips. "You did the right thing. I didn't like much hearing what you had to say, but I needed to know."

I let go of Gator's hand and reach for Delia's. "I don't want a life without you in it," I tell her.

Delia gently pulls me to my feet and leads me into the hall. "It can't ever be like it was," she says. "I won't be working for your daddy anymore. I already told him that."

"I know it can't, Delia. I already know that. Just please, *please* let me come here sometimes, maybe after school."

Delia's face softens a little. She cups my chin in her hand and narrows her eyes at me. "Were you planning to use that ax on Travis Waite tonight?"

"Were you planning to use that kitchen knife on him?"

We eye each other, like in the old days. Slow smiles creep across our faces at the same time. And we fall into a warm, familiar hug.

26

It is after one in the morning when Chase pulls the T-bird around to the back of my house and parks by the steps. Dad's two pickups are both there. He's home.

"You okay?" Chase asks.

"I'm not the one who got beat up," I say.

He runs his fingers along the back of my neck. "I mean about being back home."

I look over at him. "I don't know. A lot's going to depend on my dad, I guess."

I turn toward the house, taking in the porch, the back door, the wicker rocker, and I feel as if I've been away for a hundred years.

"Why'd you do it?" I ask. I don't have to explain. He knows I'm talking about him going against the Klan, against his dad.

He shrugs. "They were going after Gator. You know? And making trouble for the pickers. It wasn't right."

"You could've stayed out of it."

Chase doesn't say anything for a while. Maybe he's wishing he *had* looked the other way. There have been times when I've wanted to do that myself. Times when I did. Although it shames me to admit it.

When Chase turns to me, he has the strangest expression on his face. He leans over and pulls me into his arms. "Let's take off someplace," he whispers in my ear. "Leave good old Malevolence and never look back."

"*Bene*volence," I say, even though I know he said it wrong on purpose.

"Yeah, right. So are you in?"

I rub my cheek gently along the side of his face that doesn't have the gash or swollen eye, feeling his soft lips against my ear. And for one brief moment I almost say yes. I am just so happy to be with him again. But then I think about Delia and Gator and Rosemary. I think about Travis Waite still out there walking around, a free man.

"I can't leave here," I tell him.

"And I can't stay," he says.

I stare at him. I don't believe what I'm hearing.

"You know what'll happen if I stay here. Especially after last night. It's not safe for you either. But at least your dad will watch out for you. It's different with me and my dad. And there's Willy. The Klan. They'll make my life a living hell, if they don't kill me first."

His lips brush my ear. "I'm sorry, Dove."

We hold each other. The warmth from his body floods through my own. I want to keep holding on to him forever.

"You're going to graduate in a few weeks. You've got finals coming up. You can't just throw all that away," I tell him. *Or me—you can't throw me away either*, I want to say. But I don't. I lay my head on his chest.

"I'll figure something out. Maybe I can take the exams through a proctor at another school."

"Where will you go?"

He shakes his head. "I don't know. California, maybe. I know a little about growing oranges. Maybe I can get a job." He lifts a strand of my wild hair and tucks it behind my ear.

"California!" I can't believe he's going to just up and leave. "Chase, don't do this, okay? Please don't."

Chase gives me a smile full of sadness.

"There's got to be another way. Maybe you could find a place of your own over in the next county. Get a job or something." I curl up close to him. "I can't do this all by myself," I whisper. And I know he understands what I mean.

He kisses the top of my head. "I'll think about it, okay? Maybe I can stay with a friend of mine over at Florida Southern for a while."

Florida Southern is only a few miles from here, so I'm starting to feel a little more hopeful when Chase suddenly leans across me and opens the passenger door.

When I don't move, he says, "I have to go, Dove. They're probably already out looking for me. I promise I'll call you as soon as I figure out where I'll be staying."

"Someplace not too far from here," I say as I climb out of the car. "Okay?"

He gives me that lazy lopsided grin of his and shakes his head. "You make me crazy."

I stand on our back porch, watching his T-bird head down the dirt road. "I love you too," I whisper to the cloud of dust rising from his rear tires.

●　●　●　●　●　●　●　●　●　●　●　●　●　●　●　●

I sit in the rocker on the back porch for the next few hours, feeling as if I am the only person left on the planet. After a while a soft orange glow spreads along the horizon. I take off toward the groves.

I am halfway to the first row of Valencia trees when I hear the back screen door slam shut. Dad stands on the porch holding a mug of coffee in one hand. He looks over at me. I stop walking and wait for him.

He comes up beside me. "Delia phoned a few minutes ago. She told me what happened last night."

I don't say anything.

"I'm sorry, Dove. Maybe if I had been there I might have been able to stop them." Dad takes a swallow of his coffee and we start walking again.

I want to say, *But you weren't. So it happened.* Instead, I give him a shrug. "It's good you weren't there," I tell him. "I mean, I'm *glad* you weren't."

"How you holding up?"

"Fine." I start walking faster. Dad falls into step beside me.

"Chase okay?"

"Yes. No thanks to your friends." I don't tell him that Chase is thinking about leaving town. I can't bring myself to talk about that right now.

"How could you join the Klan?" I ask. "How could you *do* that?"

Dad looks away. "It's complicated," he says.

"Complicated? The Klan is about hate, Dad. You don't seem like a hateful person to me."

"It's not like that, Dove. Most of the folks in these parts, they're law-abiding, churchgoing family men. They don't want trouble," he says. "It's just lately that things have been getting out of hand. I went to a few of their meetings so I could try to talk them out of this business with Gator, but Travis and Jacob weren't having any of it. They were worried about the pickers organizing. They figured if they made an example of Gator, the others would back down. I never thought—" He takes a swallow of coffee. He doesn't finish that sentence.

I think about all the trucks and cars at Eli's last night, and how there were only a few left by the time they got to Spudder's. I want to tell my dad that God-fearing, law-abiding folks don't let the things that went on last night happen. They try to stop them. They don't look the other way. But I don't have any right to be preaching to my dad, not after that day in front of the movie theater. I have to trust that he will figure this out on his own. Maybe he already has.

"Delia say how Gator's doing?" I ask him.

"Holding his own." Dad rubs his eyes like he's got a bad headache. "I tried to get her to take him to the emergency room. I said I'd help her, but she doesn't want to move him."

"Delia told me you called her to warn her that Travis and them had Gator," I tell him.

Dad nods. He doesn't say anything. He doesn't have to. I know in my heart he's trying to make amends.

We don't talk for a while. We just walk down the road and try to keep from sinking in the softer sand.

There are still a lot of oranges on the trees. Usually most of the picking is done by now. But the slowdowns have put everything behind schedule. I don't expect any of the pickers to show up this morning. Not after what happened last night. The fruit will probably hang on the trees until it rots.

Dad reaches for an orange. He bounces it up and down in his hand a few times. "Ever hear of the golden apples guarded by the Hesperides? The ones Hercules stole?" He hands me the orange.

I shake my head. "I don't think so." I roll the orange back and forth in my palms. I like the feel of the thick, coarse skin in my hands.

"They were oranges. That's what they called oranges, golden apples. It was the fruit of the gods, the fruit of kings and emperors. It was centuries before everyday folks ever tasted one of these. Now anybody can walk into a supermarket and buy himself a can of frozen juice from golden apples, nectar that once only passed the lips of the gods."

I think about this for a minute. "It seems to me when the Lord made orange trees, He intended the fruit to be for everybody in the first place. And it's a good thing it worked out that way," I tell him. "Otherwise you'd be out of business."

Dad burps a little surprised chuckle. "You're right." His dimples deepen. A sight I haven't seen in weeks. It about snaps my heart in two. From the look of things, he is going to be out of business anyway.

I dig a hole in the orange with my thumb, peel it about halfway, and squeeze the juice into my mouth.

Dad looks over at the sunrise. "I fired Travis," he says.

"I heard."

"I'm going over to Winter Hill this morning, see if I can't hire some pickers to help finish up the season."

"Most of the crew leaders got their citrus pickers lined up when the season started. Probably only stoop laborers are left over there now," I say. "Those folks only pick row crops. They don't know anything about picking fruit. They could damage the crop without somebody overseeing them."

"I can train 'em," Dad says. "And oversee them. At least until I can find a decent crew leader."

"Decent in what way?"

We've come to an open crossroad in the groves where the produce trucks travel. The dirt is packed down harder here. "Somebody who'll treat the pickers fair," he says. He looks over at me. "You want the job?"

I can't be sure if he's teasing me or not. But then he grins, and I know he's just pulling my leg. "I'll help with the interviewing," I tell him.

He nods. "Fair enough."

"There's always Travis's crew," I say. "They won't work for him now, which means they're all out of a job."

"I don't think they'll want to work for me either."

I shrug. "Maybe if you get a good crew boss for them." In the back of my mind I'm thinking maybe Eli would like the job. Or maybe Gator, if he decides to stay around here.

We walk a little farther, not saying much. Overhead, the unpicked oranges glow like bright orange lightbulbs in the morning sun.

"Last night—none of that would have happened if I'd done something about Travis years ago. I just didn't see it." Dad stops walking to finish the rest of his coffee. "You grow up with somebody, you see them the way you always have. Travis was a hell-raiser. But I never thought he was dangerous—that he'd—" Dad shakes his head. "I thought it was an accident— But even if it was, we shouldn't have covered for him."

"It was a hit-and-run," I remind him.

Dad waves his hand back and forth. "I know. I know that."

"You going to turn him in?"

Dad lets out a little snort. "I swear you get more like your mother every day." He smiles and looks away when he says this, like some memory is lighting him up inside. When he turns back to me, he says, "You never give up, do you?"

"No."

"That's my girl."

"Well, are you?"

"I don't know, Dove. There's other folks to consider."

I know he's thinking about Travis and the Klan and what

they might do. Not to him, but to me. I put my hand on Dad's shoulder. It's not like I've forgotten about the things he has done—or didn't do. I can tell he's feeling bad about some of those things. Like me, I figure he's got his own "Adequate of Hell" to live with.

"You're right, there's other folks to consider," I say, knowing darn good and well we aren't talking about the same people.

Come Friday, I stop in the cemetery on my way home from school.
Only today I am not reading poems to dead boys. I am visiting my mother.

I have been thinking about her a lot this past week. Maybe because of what Dad said in the groves about me getting more like her every day. I don't know what that means, since I never really knew her. But I would like to find out.

Last night, after dinner, I asked Dad if we had any photos of her besides the few that made it into the family album—wedding pictures, mostly. The rest are all of me in embarrassing stages of my childhood. It turns out Dad has a whole shoe box full of photographs stashed away on his closet shelf. I dumped them out on my bed and went through every one. My mom was grinning in almost every picture. But my favorite was this photo taken at one of Spudder Rhodes's Fourth of July barbecues. I can tell it was the Fourth because there are little flags stuck in a cake on a table in the background. Spudder's wife, Nadine, makes that same cake every year.

In the photograph Mom is standing behind Spudder, pouring a bottle of soda over his head and laughing up a storm. My dad is sitting next to Spudder with this funny look on his face, kind of horrified and amused at the same time, as if he can't make up his mind how he feels about the whole thing.

It's too bad she died so young. I think I would have liked my mom. I am considering writing a special epitaph for her. I tell her this and then I spend the rest of the afternoon filling her in on what's been going on these past few weeks. Even in the telling, it's hard for me to believe all that's happened— Delia no longer working for us, Dad being in the Klan (well, maybe not for long), Travis Waite turning out to be the person who killed Gus, and Gator almost getting killed. Anybody listening to me would think I was making up a whopper.

And I tell Mom about Chase and me. I think she would have liked Chase.

Every now and then I look over my shoulder toward the woods behind the church, half expecting to see Gator and Rosemary coming toward me. But I know that won't happen. Rosemary is staying at Delia's for now, helping to take care of Gator, who's on the mend, thank goodness. I guess I'm a little jealous about Rosemary staying there. I miss Delia something awful. It's like I have this huge empty space inside me that I can't fill up. My dad misses Delia too. I can tell, although he hasn't said so. We haven't hired another house-keeper yet. We haven't even talked about it, which is fine with me. I don't want anyone else.

School has been the biggest surprise this week. The morning after Travis and them beat up Gator, not one single person in Benevolence High seemed to know about it. And they probably never will. Willy sure wasn't talking. That's how it is, I've decided. The Klan doesn't let folks know what it's up to. They really *are* the Invisible Empire, like Mr. Stone said. Besides, they're not about to let folks know there was a showdown with Delia and the pickers and the Klan backed off. So for now, school is pretty much the same. Even Willy Podd has kept out of my way. He's probably worried I will tell the whole world what happened. And maybe someday I will.

Yesterday, when I went to visit Delia and Gator, Delia told me that Jeremiah has a lawyer friend who handles civil rights cases. He's going to look into Gus's. That doesn't mean it will come to trial, but at least somebody's investigating what happened.

As for Travis Waite, he may be out of a job, but he's still hanging around. Some say he's planning to move on. Probably afraid the law will catch up with him one of these days. I hope they do, and I hope they do it before he leaves town.

If anything, things are pretty quiet around here for now. Maybe a little too quiet.

· · · · · · · · · · · · · · · · ·

When I get home, I sit down on the top step of the back porch and wait for Chase. He is staying at our place for now.

It was my dad's idea. He flat out asked me that morning in the groves what Chase planned to do. I guess he knew Jacob most likely wouldn't let him back in the house. He was right about that.

Chase was staying with that friend of his who graduated last year and is going to Florida Southern College, not far from here. He called me the night after he left town to tell me where he was. My dad said to tell Chase he needed someone to help Eli with the pickers, if Chase was interested. So Chase came back, for now, anyway. Jacob Tully has got to be mad as blazes about that. I smile every time I think about it.

The pickers had no problem coming back to work when they heard Eli was going to oversee things. But Eli's not too steady on his feet these days. Chase—he's Eli's legs for now. He works in the groves every day after school. Sort of like an assistant crew boss. Although it's just for the rest of this season. Eli and Chase take only a small percentage for each crate the pickers fill. And they don't withhold money to pay off bills at the camp store. Now the pickers have money in their pockets and can buy their groceries wherever they please, and they don't have to pay three times more than they would someplace else. So I don't expect Travis will have that camp store for much longer.

Every evening since he came here, Chase comes in from the groves to spend a little time with me before dinner. I have an ice-cold pitcher of lemonade waiting for him, like I do now. And while he's drinking it, I read him poems. I've been reading *Howl* to him. Every so often I look up. He's watching me, and he's listening. So far his eyes haven't glazed over once. I thought this might be because I told him the school board banned the book. I figured that might get his attention. But then yesterday Chase surprised me.

He said, "This is good stuff, Dove. Raw. You know? I like it."

At first I thought he was talking about my lemonade. But then he pointed to the book. I felt a little something stir in that empty space inside me when he said that.

The ice cubes are starting to melt in the pitcher of lemonade. I see someone coming toward me from the groves. At first I think it's Chase, but when I squint harder I see it's my dad. He's been spending a lot of time out there this week, helping Chase and Eli.

Dad and I, we're being real careful with each other these days. It won't ever be the same between us. But maybe that's not such a bad thing. We never used to talk much. My dad's idea of good parenting was to make sure I got my allowance every Saturday. It's different now. Not better. Not worse. Just different.

Dad sits on the step next to me.

"Chase is doing a fine job," he says.

I nod. "That's good."

"You heard anything more about Gator?"

"He's a little better. I was over at Delia's yesterday. He was sitting up, reading." I look over at Dad. "His face is still a mess, though. You know, from the belt buckle."

It's Dad's turn to nod. "I've set up a special pension fund for Delia," Dad says.

"Meaning what?"

"Money she can retire on, if she wants. It should be enough to take good care of her in her old age."

"She won't take it," I tell him. I am afraid Dad might be

trying to bribe Delia not to say anything to the law about what happened to Gus.

"It's not a gift, Dove." He looks over at me, then frowns. "Or a bribe, if that's what you're thinking."

I look away.

"Delia earned this money. It's like anybody working for a company. The company provides the workers with a pension when they retire."

"Well, that's good, then," I say. I'm relieved Delia won't have to go on cleaning houses for the rest of her born days. Although I know Jeremiah would take care of her.

A cool breeze rustles the leaves of the orange trees and sends the scent of Valencia blossoms our way. I lift my face and breathe in the air.

"Well, will you look at that," Dad says. He points toward the sky. "A whooping crane. I'll be darned. Those things are really rare around these parts."

I shade my eyes with my hands, watching the bird. With the sunlight glinting off its glorious white wings—wings tipped with black feathers—it looks like an angel flying over-head.

Dad and I sit there, gaping in awe, knowing we will probably never see such a sight again for as long as we live. And when I glance back down to earth, with the sun still blurring my vision, I think I see, for the tiniest minute, Chase and Gator laughing and running between the orange trees, kicking up sandy soil with their bare feet, just like we used to do, back when we were kids.

Acknowledgments

As often happens, this book began as something quite different several years ago. I have been fortunate to have had a number of people with me throughout its sometimes surprising evolution. They have all made this a memorable journey.

My thanks to friends who, over the years, have read and commented on other versions of this book: Laurie Halse Anderson, Elizabeth Bennett-Bailey, Pat Brisson, Denise Brunkus, Dorothy Carey, Nancy Evans Cooney, Paula DePaolo, Joan Elste, Judy Freeman, Deborah Heiligman, Martha Hewson, Sally Keehn, Susan Korman, Trinka Hakes Noble, Margie Palatini, Wendy Pfeffer, Penny Pollock (who never stopped believing in this book), Shirley Roffman, Pamela Curtis Swallow, Virginia Troeger, Laura Whipple, Kay Winters, and Elvira Woodruff.

My gratitude to Karen Wojtyla, whose suggestions and encouragement gave me the courage to take the original story in a new and more challenging direction.

My deepest appreciation to my editor, Wendy Loggia, whose guidance and support have been invaluable; to her assistant, Emily Jacobs, who is always so thoughtful; to my agent, Tracey Adams, for her constant encouragement; and to Christina Biamonte for reading and commenting on a later draft of this book.

Special thanks to Darryl McDonald, who spent hours taking slides of orange groves, migrant workers, and migrant housing to share with me when I couldn't get back to Florida before my deadline.

My heartfelt gratitude to my husband, Mac, who was born and raised in central Florida, and without whom I would never have known that mustard greens *don't* grow in cypress swamps, sandspurs are like nettles, and swamp cabbage is just your garden-variety hearts of palm.

Joyce McDonald earned bachelor's and master's degrees in English from the University of Iowa and a Ph.D. in English from Drew University. She is the author of many outstanding novels for teens, including *Swallowing Stones,* an ALA Top Ten Best Book for Young Adults; *Shadow People,* a New York Public Library Book for the Teen Age; and *Shades of Simon Gray,* an ALA Best Book for Young Adults and a nominee for the Edgar Allan Poe Award. Joyce McDonald lives in a quiet rural town in northwestern New Jersey with her husband and their cats. While she's never actually read poems in cemeteries, she does share Dove's passion for poetry.